The Payback Murders

Other book by Jane Aldlen

The Crystal's Curse

Jobyna's Blues

Across A Crowded Room

The Payback Murders

Jane Alden

Desert Palm Press

The Payback Murders

By Jane Alden

©2021 Jane Alden

ISBN (book): 9781954213128
ISBN (epub): 9781954213135

Desert Palm Press
1961 Main Street, Suite 220
Watsonville, California 95076
www.desertpalmpress.com

Editor: Heather Flournoy
Cover Design: TreeHouse Studio

Printed in the United States of America
First Edition July 2021

Acknowledgements

Attorney August Mapes showed up briefly in my first book, Across A Crowded Room. She's been waiting, sometimes patiently, sometimes shifting from foot to foot, to tell her own story. The Payback Murders gives August a platform. I hope you enjoy getting to know her.

My friend, Deputy District Attorney (Ret.) Jennifer Dawson, was an invaluable source of information about how police would handle evidence. She also sits still while I read each of my manuscripts aloud before submitting them for editing. My editor, Heather Flournoy, is wonderful; thorough, insightful, and so smart. Again, a special cover by the amazing renaissance woman, Ann McMan.

Many, many thanks to Lee Fitzsimmons, publisher at Desert Palm Press, for always doing what she says she'll do.

Chapter One

AUGUST MAPES'S ATTENTION DRIFTED from the open file folder on her desk. Fall was in the air, just a hint of chill and the smell of burning leaves. The squeals of children playing in the fountain in Washington Square flowed across the street to her office and into open windows. She turned the pages of notes from the Grant case looking for anything she could have done differently.

Lena Potter stuck her head in August's office door. "It's one o'clock. Let me make you some lunch." The nameplate on Lena's desk in the front office read 'Secretary,' but the word was inadequate. August had tried suggesting a different title when they moved into the office, but Lena refused. "I'm a secretary and a very good one, and I'm proud of it."

"Of course, but you're so much more. A friend, confidant, handler, supporter..."

That day, five years before, Lena had dismissed the talk with a wave of her hand and had resumed setting up files for August's fledgling private law practice.

"If you're driving to Lake Placid today, you should start with a full stomach. You've got dark circles under your eyes."

August turned to look at her reflection in the window behind her and smoothed a stray hair. "I know. I look like crap." She picked up the file. "The Grant case took all the starch out of me. It will be a while before I shake the look on Bennie Grant's face when the judge gave her husband full custody of their daughter."

Lena nodded. "I know how hard you worked for her." She leaned over the desk and patted August's hand. "So, what's your pleasure? Soup, sandwich, or Lena's Special of the Day, half and half?"

"Soup. And I'll eat here at my desk. I want to get this file closed before I leave."

Lena went to the door, pushed it shut, and leaned against it. "I'm onto what you're doing, you know. You're poring over the Grant case and asking yourself if you could have done anything differently to get a better outcome."

"That's exactly what I'm doing. You know me too well."

"You couldn't have. That judge made up his mind from the beginning he was going to go with the father and grandmother. You were able to get regular visits for the mother. That was a victory."

"And where did you go to law school?"

"I don't need a law degree. I know you." She put out her hand. "Give it."

August picked up the file, closed the cover, and passed it over.

"Tomato soup with crackers and an ice-cold glass of milk, coming up."

"I love you, Lena."

Lena nodded. "I know."

August checked her watch. Her packed bags waited upstairs in her apartment. If she ate fast, she could be on the road by 2:00 and in Lake Placid by 7:30, just before dark. She thumbed through a stack of back issues of law journals. She looked at the dates and shook her head. They'd been piling up for months, from August 1951 to the latest one, September 1952. She'd been saving them with the best of intentions, but with the Grant case on top of all her other clients, she never seemed to get around to reading them. She pulled out a few that looked interesting. She could use the vacation time catching up on at least some of her professional reading. She hoped to even sneak in a good mystery novel or two.

Outside in the front office, the phone on Lena's desk jangled. Lena stuck her head in the door again. "There's a woman on the phone asking to talk with you. I've tried putting her off, but she's very insistent."

August looked at her watch again and groaned.

"She says June referred her."

June Fleming was August's ex. "Did she say what it's about? Can it wait two weeks?"

"She sounds rather desperate."

August sighed and shook her head. "I'll give her a few minutes while you heat the soup, but I won't be at my best dealing with desperation right now." She took a breath and told herself to be careful to keep impatience out of her voice. It would only make things worse. She picked up the blinking phone line. "This is August Mapes."

"Miss Mapes, thank you so much for agreeing to talk to me. Your secretary was kind to me and protective of you at the same time. Not easy when she has a practically hysterical woman on the line. I don't want you to think of me that way."

"Yes, Lena is one of a kind." She tucked the receiver between her ear and shoulder, dug her hands in her pockets, and paced. The woman's emotions sounded under control, but August heard anxiety just under the surface. "How can I help you, Miss..."

"Kathleen O'Brien. June Fleming gave me your contact information. She speaks very highly of you."

"That's nice to hear. The truth is, Miss O'Brien, I'm just leaving for a two-week trip. If you tell me the nature of your problem, perhaps I can recommend a colleague."

"Two weeks?"

August was used to hearing desperation in the voices of her clients. She recognized Kathleen O'Brien's anxiety had accelerated to near panic. Again, a painful memory of Bennie Grant flashed across her mind. She sat down. "Tell me what's going on."

"I can't tell you on the phone. Is there any way we can meet, just for a few minutes?"

August checked her watch for the third time. 1:30. "I can give you a few minutes if you come right over and you don't mind a lawyer in jeans and a flannel shirt. My office is at—"

"I know your address. The thing is, I'm...not able...to come there. Could you possibly come to my apartment? I'm just two blocks south of the square at 153 Bleecker, three minutes' walk from you."

Unbelievable! A frantic disabled woman with a secret problem. Just the thing to appeal to your Wonder Woman complex, Mapes. Your urge to rescue damsels in distress. "Twenty minutes. I can give you twenty minutes." She hung up the phone, grabbed a legal pad and pencil, and ran through the outer office. "Lena, hold the soup till I get back."

August jogged across Washington Square North then speed-walked into the park. The day was overcast, threatening rain. She rushed past two men on a bench.

"Hey, girlie."

She paused and looked around. "Me?"

"Yeah." One man held up a paper bag crumpled into the shape of the bottle inside. "Want a drink?"

Crutches leaned against the bench, and his left pant leg hung empty below the knee.

He patted his thigh. "Don't let this scare you. Lost it in the Philippines." He gestured with the bag again. "Have a drink."

"Thank you, but I'm in a rush."

The other man spoke up. "Leave her alone, Frank."

August hesitated, then turned away and started back down the path.

"Stuck up bitch."

August glanced back over her shoulder. She struggled with competing emotions: pity that the man had suffered a devastating wound in the war and anger that he felt entitled to disrespect her.

She exited the park and paused at the front door of Kathleen O'Brien's apartment building to get her breathing under control. She buzzed the fourth floor apartment. The intercom popped. "Yes?"

"It's August Mapes, Miss O'Brien."

"I'll be right down."

The woman appeared on the stairs and opened the front door. She was striking, with porcelain skin and thick auburn hair falling in waves to her shoulders. She wore a simple green linen sheath matching the color of her eyes. "Thank you so much for coming. Do you mind the stairs? There's an elevator, but it's one of those freight things out of service more often than not. I don't mind. I prefer the stairs anyway." She looked August up and down and smiled. "You look fit enough for a few stairs."

August reflexively tucked in her shirt. She felt herself color under the woman's scrutiny. "Excuse my showing up dressed like a lumberjack. As I said on the phone, I'm leaving in a few minutes for a road trip." She gestured toward the stairs. "This way?"

They climbed the three flights. "I've passed this building a million times, but I've never been inside."

August looked around the apartment, a converted loft with a high ceiling, exposed brick walls, and original oak hardwood floors glowing under the light from large windows facing Bleecker. August noticed an open rolltop desk against one wall holding a typewriter and neatly stacked pages. The entire north wall was covered floor to ceiling with shelves full of thick, hardbound reference books.

"Your place is amazing."

"Do you like it? The building was a button factory in the eighteen hundreds, and this top floor was the warehouse." She pointed to a large glass jar on the kitchen counter filled with buttons. "I find old buttons all the time in cracks and crevices."

"It's charming."

"I spend most of my time here, so I've tried making the place as comfortable as possible." Kathleen gestured toward the desk. "As you can see, it's both my home and my work space."

"I can tell. You have your own personal reference library."

"Yes, a big part of my work involves research."

An antique grandfather clock in the corner chimed the three-quarter hour. August checked her watch. "Can we get started?"

"Of course. I know your time is short." Kathleen O'Brien gestured toward the sofa and took a straight chair nearby. Two legal-sized manila envelopes lay on the coffee table.

August rested her tablet on her lap. "Tell me why you called."

Kathleen sat up straight with her hands folded. "First, I apologize for sounding like an overexcited woman on the phone. I hate that kind of weakness." She clutched her hands together tightly, making her knuckles go white, and cleared her throat. "I'm a freelance book editor. Most of my business comes as referrals from small and mid-sized publishing houses needing occasional help with overflow workload. Sometimes, though, an author contacts me directly. Usually they've read a book I've edited and perceive I can help them get their work ready for submission to agents and publishers. I have to admit most of them wouldn't get a second look without my help. Do I sound smug? Anyway, I wasn't surprised when this came in the mail." She picked up one of the manila envelopes from the coffee table and handed it to August.

Kathleen's address was neatly hand-lettered on the envelope. The return address was E. Gamin, Box 352, Grand Central Station. The envelope was postmarked New York City two weeks before. August pulled several typewritten pages from the envelope. The top page was a brief, typed letter.

Dear Miss O'Brien:

I hope you will excuse my sending the enclosed first chapter of my book to you directly without an introduction. I am a fan of your work. I've read several books for which you served as the editor, and I believe you are the ideal person to help make my story the best it can be. I hope you won't find me immodest if I tell you I'm very proud of the work so far.

You will also find enclosed a money order in the amount of $500. I believe the payment will more than cover your customary fee. If this amount is insufficient, please tell me. I know your time is very valuable, and well worth it.

I look forward to a mutually satisfying professional relationship.
Very truly yours,
E. Gamin

August flipped through the next four pages. The first two had blue pencil editing marks, and the last two were without marks. "Should I read this?"

Kathleen nodded.

Dan Efram

He always took the same bar stool and ordered the same scotch, double and neat. The bartender didn't even ask anymore, just gently slid a linen drink napkin in front of him and placed the crystal glass in the square's middle. The Oak Room knew how to cater to its regulars. I chose my usual table in the corner, close enough to watch him and far enough away to escape his notice. Once I had satisfied myself three weeks ago he was the right man, thanks to my research in the New York Times *morgue,* I began Phase I, tracking his routine. I had observed him every weekday evening for the last two weeks.

He didn't know his choice of the Oak Room was perfect for my purposes. Not too big, but not too intimate. Airy, with nice high ceilings. In the late afternoon, there were only a few customers, but the bar stools and tables would begin filling soon with commuting businessmen, killing time until they boarded trains for New Jersey or Connecticut.

He never met a friend or colleague, or even spoke to anyone. He had one mission: downing three double scotches before catching the 6:15 Ridgewood train. That took focus.

I nursed a vodka and tonic. Time to begin Phase II—detailed planning for the actual event. Driving in rush hour traffic from midtown Manhattan to New Jersey required a clear head. I would beat his train to Ridgewood station, observe him disembark, and follow him to his house at 315 Murray Avenue. I took a quick sip of my drink to cover an involuntary smile.

My mind wandered. Nothing new to see now. He was halfway through scotch number two. I checked my watch. On schedule. I looked across Central Park South. Hansom cab drivers coaxed their horses into line waiting for customers wanting a twilight ride through the park, just like in the movies. A couple boarded the first cab in line. She looked all smiles and he looked worried, as though *something was expected of him that he might not be able to discern.*

Dan signaled the bartender for his third drink. My cue. I caught the waiter's eye and opened my briefcase for my wallet. The back of my hand brushed a small oblong leather case. I wouldn't need it yet. It would come into play in Phase III.

I went through the hotel lobby and out the front door. The doorman called for my car. I pulled on my driving gloves, checked my watch, and headed across town to the Lincoln Tunnel under the river to New Jersey, then turned north toward Bergen County and the township of Ridgewood. Traffic was lighter than I expected. I had allowed a full hour for the trip, and in only fifty-one minutes I was parked in the Ridgewood commuter parking lot with a line of sight to arriving trains.

Two cars with women drivers pulled into the lot and parked next to each other close to the station platform. I figured they were wives of men on the train. One of them got out of her car and leaned against the driver's side of the other, chatting through the open window. She threw her head back and laughed loudly. I wondered if she or the other woman was his wife, Gloria. I learned about her in the Times *morgue. She might complicate Phase III.*

Five minutes behind schedule, the train pulled into Ridgewood station. A dozen men filed down the steps and headed for the parking lot. Two, neither of them Dan, joined the chatting women.

I had begun thinking he missed the train when he appeared and headed for his car in the lot. People who are used to being drunk walk with a distinctive exaggerated steadiness. He'd probably had at least one more drink on the train. Maybe two. His tie was still neatly knotted. He carried a briefcase in his right hand and a folded newspaper under his left arm.

Murray Avenue was a mile and a half from the station, through the village and northwest. Streetlights lining Main Street flickered on in the deepening twilight. We passed shops lit up for the evening trade, the white steeple of the First Presbyterian Church, and the Ridgewood police headquarters. He turned left onto a street winding through a quiet, established neighborhood with large lots, a canopy of mature trees, and no sidewalks, all good for my Phase III purposes. There would be few casual passersby. He drove slowly, with exaggerated care. Tailing him was difficult without looking like a float in a slowly moving parade, so I pulled to the shoulder and waited for some separation between our cars.

Down the street, he turned left into the brick driveway of an attractive Norman Tudor house. I stopped across the street and shut off my lights and engine.

The house had stone trim, half-timbers, and two round turrets at the entrance. There were two chimneys, a large one in the front, probably a formal living room, and a small one in the back, a den or library. His headlights illuminated an attached two-car garage on the left side of the house. There were no lights on inside. Where was Gloria? He left the car running, got out to lift the garage door, pulled in, and closed the door.

He turned on a light in the room next to the garage, the kitchen. He opened a cabinet, took down a glass, and left the room. He'd be drinking his dinner. A light came on in the back of the house. I checked my watch. 8:05. Nothing more to see tonight. I needed to learn more about his wife.

***

The next morning, I called his house. After three rings, a female voice with an accent came on the line. "Efram's residence."

"Mrs. Efram, please."

"No Mrs. Efram here."

"This is her insurance agent. It's very important I get in touch with her. Do you know how I can speak with her?"

"No Mrs. Efram here. Goodbye." She hung up.

A maid? Is she a live-in?

I had planned to skip the Oak Room bar and drive directly to Ridgewood in the late afternoon to wait for his train, but now I needed to go to New Jersey earlier to find out about the maid. I took the bridge instead of the tunnel this time across the Hudson *at Fort Lee and turned north into Bergen County. I arrived in front of the Murray Avenue house at 3:00, parked across the street, and waited.*

At four on the dot, a middle-aged woman wearing a maid's uniform under her light coat, carrying a purse and a shopping bag, came out the front door and locked it behind her. I followed her on foot to a bus stop. She sat on the bench beside a younger woman. I stood behind them, leaning against the side of the shelter.

She arranged her bag and purse at her feet. "Hello, Greta."

"Marta."

They looked up the street in unison. Marta fussed some more with her bag. "Maybe the bus will come on time today."

Greta, the younger woman, blew out a tired sigh. "Maybe." She looked up the street again. "I envy you. You have no messy children to clean up after. I no sooner get the kitchen floor done than they track in dirt and mud. And the missus just looks at me like she's daring me to complain."

"Be glad you don't have a dog."

That got my attention. Did Dan have a dog?

"But Mrs. Efram took it with her when she left, didn't she?"

"Yes, thank God. She didn't want to, but she said she didn't trust him to keep the thing alive." Marta gathered her bag and purse. "The bus comes."

I stepped behind the shelter and watched the two women board the bus. It pulled away from the curb, belching a black cloud of diesel smoke.

I walked back to my car with a spring in my step. There would be no wife or dog to complicate things. I looked up and down the deserted street and considered taking advantage of the waning daylight to reconnoiter. Better not approach from the front and risk some self-appointed lookout behind her front window curtain alerting Dan to a stranger snooping around. I drove to the rear of the property. Houses on the south side of Murray Avenue adjoined undeveloped sweet gum woods. The leaves were already starting to show fall colors. I hiked through the strip of trees and crossed Dan's back lawn. A door led into the garage. It was unlocked. Did the maid accidently leave the door open, or was this Dan's habit? Whatever, my Phase III strategy was clear. I would enter the garage, wait for him to pull in, and make my move before he got out of the car to shut the garage door behind him. No need to wrestle his body, which would be dead weight by then, back into the car seat.

I backtracked through the woods and drove down Main Street again, past the police station, the church, and the Ridgewood National Bank. A clock in front of the bank said 5:20. Two hours till Dan's train arrived. I bought a coffee to go at the Bergen Diner and a local newspaper from a vending machine on the street corner and drove to the train station parking lot to wait.

The train station scene was a replay of the night before, except only one of the two women showed up for her husband. When Dan appeared, she called his name and waved to him. I expected he might stop and talk with her, but he returned the wave and walked to his car. Tailing him was easier because I knew where we were headed. I lagged behind when he turned on Murray Avenue. Just like the night before, he pulled up to the garage, got out with the motor running to open the garage door, went back to his car, drove in, then lowered the door from the inside.

I lifted my briefcase from the passenger's seat onto my lap. I watched my fingers fumble on the latch as though they belonged to someone else. Not the time for nerves. Turn those feelings into anticipation and excitement. I took out the small leather case and unsnapped it. Two etorphine hydrochloride syringes. Fast acting and long lasting. Vets use the drug to immobilize large wild game animals. My plan was complete. Tomorrow it would be time to implement Phase III.

***

The following night at seven o'clock, I parked on Main Street in front of the church and pulled the duffel bag from the trunk. I jogged to Murray Avenue and crept through the woods behind the *house and across the back lawn. The garage door was unlocked, just as before. My luck was holding. By 7:15, I was in the garage laying out my tools: rubber gloves, duct tape, a garden hose, and two etorphine hydrochloride syringes, a primary and a backup. I didn't expect to need the extra one, but better to be safe than sorry. I found a spot in the corner near the garage door and settled in to wait.*

You can tell a lot about a man from his garage. The space was neat enough but gave the impression of disuse and the absence of stuff rather than any organizational plan. For example, how many ladders a man owns tells a story about him, how handy he is and how prepared for the everyday little things that go wrong in a house. Dan didn't have ladders. One wall of the garage was entirely covered by a peg board with hooks to hold tools. Each hook had an outline of the tool meant to hang on it, like the tracing police draw around the body of a murder victim. A few tools hung on the hooks here and there—a saw, a hammer, hedge clippers—but not in their designated spots. The garage represented a man with his life falling apart. Maybe I was doing him a favor.

I checked my own tools again. I pulled on my gloves and took the cap off one of the syringe needles and pushed the plunger just enough to release a squirt of liquid. I felt confident with the syringe. I had practiced by injecting an orange. I checked my watch. He could pull up any second. I closed my eyes and ran a mental movie of the scene.

In my internal movie, the sound of the engine signals his turning into the driveway. Headlights shine on the garage door, outlining the edges. The car door opens, he raises the garage door and gets back in the car and pulls into the garage. The enclosed space amplifies the engine noise. I smell the engine, an intoxicating odor transporting me back to my grandpa's farm. My cousin and I taking the gas cap off Grandpa's pickup truck and getting a rush sniffing the fumes.

Then I heard Dan's car for real. The car door opened, and the garage door swung up. Headlights lit the inside of the garage. I backed farther into my corner to avoid the light and accidently kicked the roll of duct tape into the open. It circled around in a spiral. I held my breath. He might notice. He got back in the car, pulled into the garage, turned off the lights and engine, and opened the car door. I sprang. The needle went in his neck just above the shirt collar. He turned with a look more annoyed than afraid, then slumped over the steering wheel onto the horn, blasting an alarm into the quiet street. A lookout peeking through her window would certainly hear the noise. I pushed his limp body back against the seat, pulled down the garage door, and waited, listening. The faint hoot of an owl in the backyard. No sounds from the street.

I found the duct tape under the car, unwound the garden hose, and fed one end into the car's exhaust pipe. I wrapped the connection between the hose and the pipe carefully. The tape would need to hold several hours. Would a man prepare this carefully to kill himself?

I checked his pulse. Slow but steady. I had imagined his eyes closed, but he stared fixedly straight ahead, unblinking. I wondered if he heard all my preparations and was just unable to react. Did I hope so? Maybe.

A disgusting trickle of spittle glistened at the corner of his mouth.

I stuck the other end of the hose through the back window, rolled up the glass to hold the hose in place, and taped it for good measure. I reached across his body and turned the ignition key. The motor started right up. I checked the gas level. Three quarters of a tank. I had hoped for at least half a tank. A bonus and more good luck.

I gathered up my bag with the syringes inside and checked the floor in the corner and near the garage door and the car for footprints. I turned at the back door, surveyed the scene once again, and left.

August looked up from the last paragraph.

Kathleen took the pages from her. "What do you think?"

"I'm no editor. He seems to have a good grasp of grammar and punctuation."

Kathleen nodded. "But you're thinking of copy editors. They come along later in the process. They pay attention to spelling, grammar, word usage, and so on. I'm a developmental editor. I work with the author on big picture issues like plot consistency and character motivation and behavior. What do you think about the piece in general?"

August looked over the typed pages again. "Aside from the disturbing subject matter, which is hard to read, the main character seems to move through the world as though he's invisible, no human interaction at all. Maybe it's what the author had in mind." She shrugged. "As I said, I'm no editor."

Kathleen took the pages back. "I agree it's disturbing. I decided to decline. I sent Mr. Gamin a letter returning his money order and telling him I'm too busy with other work. That part is true." She gestured toward the desk. "I'm knee-deep in editing a rather dense philosophy textbook for Summit Press.

"I considered recommending one or two other editors, but I honestly feel so repulsed by the story that I didn't want anything more to do with him. I went back to my textbook editing and forgot about Mr. Gamin. Yesterday, this came."

She handed August the second manila envelope. It bore Kathleen's address neatly hand-lettered, the same as the first envelope, but with a different return address, a post office box at Pennsylvania Station this time. The postmark was New York City. August shook out two newspaper clippings and a money order for $1000.

The first clipping was dated May 24, 1932 from the New Canaan, Connecticut *Daily Voice*, twenty years before. The headline read "New Canaan Youth Sentenced For Hit-and-Run Deaths." There were several photographs. The first showed two horribly smashed cars. The next was a family grouping of a man and woman with a little auburn-haired girl, and underneath was the caption: "Mr. and Mrs. William O'Brien and their daughter Kathleen."

Below the family picture were two high school graduation shots. The first was labeled David Gates, Driver, and the second was a pretty girl identified as Sarah Franks, Deceased.

August looked up. "The child in the picture is you."

"Yes. Twenty years ago, a carful of drunk young people, celebrating the eighteenth birthday of the driver ran a stoplight and killed my parents. I was nine years old, asleep in the back seat. The driver fled the scene, leaving my parents bleeding to death."

August shivered. "And you?"

"I stayed in the hospital for a few days with a concussion and this." She pulled back her hair to reveal a jagged three-inch scar along the hairline, marring her otherwise flawless skin.

August read the article under the photos. A jury convicted David Gates, the driver, of involuntary manslaughter. The judge sentenced him to six months in prison, citing mitigating circumstances in his sentencing. Mr. Gates was about to start college with the intention of going on to medical school. The accident was his first offense. The passengers in the car distracted him, causing him to miss the red stop light. The newspaper reporter chased down the judge for a quote. "Several lives are already ruined. I can't see how ruining another serves any purpose."

August shook her head. "A slap on the wrist." She studied Kathleen's face for a reaction to the details of the loss of her parents. "Reliving the accident must be painful for you."

Kathleen touched the scar. "I don't remember anything about the accident or the hospital, or very much about the following weeks."

She gestured toward the second newspaper clipping. "Read the next one. It's dated a few days ago."

It was a recent article from the same New Canaan paper, dated two weeks before. "New Canaan Man Dies, Apparent Suicide." There was a photograph of the death scene, the front of an attractive house with stone trim, half-timbers, and two round turrets at the entrance.

August looked up. "This is the house described in the story." She read the two brief paragraphs below the photograph.

Neighbors called police to a private home on Mulberry Road. They found David Gates, 40, a longtime New Canaan resident, dead of apparent carbon monoxide poisoning.

An informant, who declined to be identified, told reporters Gates seemed despondent over a separation from his wife.

August picked up the money order. "A thousand dollars this time. Was there a note from E. Gamin?"

Kathleen shook her head.

August put the clippings and money order back in the manila envelope. "The story's names and town are different, but the connections are clear. There must be some link between you and the author. A minute ago, you said you sent the first money order back to Mr. Gamin. How do you know your author is a man? Do you have some idea of the identity?"

Kathleen stammered. "I don't know. I guess I just picture the author as a man. I do that. I tend to get an image of the author I'm editing. I have no idea who he might be."

"Have you called the police?"

"No."

"Is that why you contacted me? You want me to go with you to the police?"

Kathleen pushed up from her chair. "Where are my manners? I should have offered you something to drink. Iced tea or water?"

"Water is fine."

She took her time filling tumblers with ice cubes and water.

August peeked at her watch. 2:15 already. She felt her prospect of reaching Lake Placid before dark slipping away. She tamped down an urge to feel angry with Kathleen. The disruption of her plans was her own fault. Damn Wonder Woman! "So, what about the police?"

Kathleen placed the two glasses on the coffee table. "I called you because I can't go to the police." She sat and drank from the glass. "Have you heard of a condition called agoraphobia?"

"Yes, heard of it, but I'm not an expert by any means. The term is Greek for 'a fear of the marketplace,' right?"

"Right, but the reality of the condition isn't that simple. It should be called phobiaphobia, a fear of fear. People with this..." She glanced at August. "...disability are paralyzed by the possibility of having a panic attack without any way of escaping or getting help. We avoid public transportation, standing in lines, elevators, bridges. Both open spaces and closed spaces."

Her confession about her disability explained the stairs instead of the freight elevator. August made a note on her legal pad. "And I think I've read people with agoraphobia can't leave their homes."

"That's the common understanding of it, but it's not entirely true. For five years, since my first panic attack, I've had to plan very carefully where I go. I feel safest here in my home, but I can go a few other places like the park and to my local bodega on the corner. It's better if I'm with a person I trust."

"I'm a bit unclear about why June would refer your case to me. This isn't my area of practice. If you somehow get embroiled in a murder case, you're going to need a good criminal attorney."

Kathleen looked beseechingly into her eyes. "June told me you often work with a very skilled private investigator. Can't you help me find out more information about E. Gamin? Then you could get the police to come to me here in my apartment. I doubt they would take me seriously with only a chapter of fiction and a newspaper clipping as evidence. What if the whole thing is just a coincidence?"

"We need to tell the police as soon as possible." August heard herself say 'we.' Was she already thinking of this woman as her client? "You may be in danger. This person knows where you live."

Kathleen folded her arms and hugged herself. "No, I simply can't go to the police." She got up and went to the window and stared out. "Maybe it's best to wait and see. Maybe the story is just made up."

August blew out a breath. She didn't have time for this now. "I'll be gone two weeks. I'll have my detective work on finding E. Gamin. When I come back to town, we'll talk to the police. In the meantime, give me everything: the clippings, the money order, and the typed pages. We may find clues in the story to help identify E. Gamin. My secretary will type a copy of the pages and messenger them to you. Finish editing the chapter and send it back to the Penn Station post office box. We need to keep a connection with him. Do not cash the money order."

She gathered up her legal tablet and the two manila envelopes. "Now I really must go. I'll call you in two weeks."

Kathleen walked her down the stairs to the front door. "Thank you so much. You're all June said."

"Speaking of June, how do you know her?"

"Her family and mine lived in the same New Canaan neighborhood. She was my babysitter. I had a huge crush on her. Still do a bit, I guess. My memory of her, anyway. I haven't seen her since my parents died. I knew she had become a lawyer and I found her through the New York Bar Association. She's a tax attorney...of course you know that."

"I'll get my investigator started on finding E. Gamin. You should be thinking about finding a good criminal attorney, if things move in that direction." She turned to go.

"Miss Mapes, I feel so much better. Thank you." She embraced August and held on like a drowning woman who had just found a life preserver floating by.

August twisted out of the embrace and stepped backward. "I'll be in touch in two weeks."

She retraced her path across the park. The bench where the two men had sat was empty. She slowed her pace. No need to hurry back to her office. She had decided to wait till the next morning for the drive to Lake Placid. She'd miss only a few hours of her vacation. Traffic would be light if she left early.

When August came in the office door, Lena looked up from her typewriter. "You know how late it is, right? You'll never get there before dark even if you leave this minute."

"I know, I know. I'm going to wait till tomorrow. Right now, please call the Grigsby's and tell them I'll be there tomorrow around one o'clock. They may be rushing to get the place opened for me. No sense putting them out unnecessarily. After you call Lake Placid, get Blackie Rye on the phone."

"Why do we need a private investigator just before you leave for two weeks off?"

"I want to get him going on something while I'm out of town."

Blackie, short for Blackwell Rye, a retired NYPD detective, was the best in the business at finding assets when her clients' husbands tried to hide them from the court. Maybe he could use those skills and contacts to find E. Gamin while she was in Lake Placid. Lena buzzed August with Rye on the line.

"Blackie, Lena's sending you something. I'll be gone for two weeks, but I'm hoping you can get started while I'm away. It may be a wild goose chase, but if anyone can make heads or tails of it, it's you."

"Certainly. Another deadbeat trying to hide his money?"

"This one's a bit different. Lena will send you a note describing the situation."

"I'll get started on it apace."

She hung up and scribbled a note to Blackie. "Assume this is a fictionalized account of a real murder. See what you can find out about E Gamin while I'm gone. We'll talk when I'm back." She pulled the typewritten pages and the newspaper clippings from the manila envelopes and took them to Lena's desk. "Make two copies of the typed pages. One goes to Blackie with my note and the newspaper clippings, and one set of the pages goes to Miss O'Brien."

"Should I start a client file?"

August considered the question. She felt herself being sucked into a situation that had every possibility of turning out badly. The story might be just a story. Kathleen O'Brien might be more in need of a psychiatrist for her agoraphobia than a lawyer. Would she really be able to help this woman? She shook her head. "Don't open a file yet."

She dropped into her desk chair and flipped through the notes from her talk with Kathleen. Thanks to June, instead of sitting on her sleeping porch overlooking Lake Placid reading a murder mystery as she had planned, August suspected she was in danger of becoming a character in one.

Chapter Two

AUGUST DROVE UP MAIN Street in Lake Placid, past faux-Alpine storefronts dating back twenty years, when the 1932 Winter Olympics put the sleepy village on the map. There were plenty of vacant parking spots to choose from. She pulled into a space in front of the Stop 'N Shop, got out of the car, and lifted her face to the warmth of the sun. This time of the year was the best in the resort town. All the summer tourists left after Labor Day, and the first snow was still weeks away.

She took down the top of her Austin-Healey, white with a red leather interior. A teenaged boy passing on the sidewalk whistled and gave her a thumbs-up. "Nice car!"

"Thanks."

A tiny brass bell tinkled when she pushed through the front door of the grocery shop. The Grigsby's, caretakers for the cabin, would have laid in basic supplies like coffee and some breakfast items, but she wanted to pick up a few bottles of Finger Lakes wines. The elderly man behind the counter looked up from the book he was reading. "Help you?"

"I'm after some wine."

He looked her up and down. "I'll wager you know more about good wine than I do. Help yourself." He gestured toward the back of the store and returned to his book.

She chose two bottles of Sauvignon Blanc and a Cabernet and took them to the counter. She smiled at the title of his book, *The Adventures of Sherlock Holmes*.

She pulled out her checkbook to pay for the wine. "So, you like mysteries?"

"That Sherlock Holmes was something, wasn't he?"

"Yes, he was." She could certainly use Sherlock Holmes right now on the O'Brien case.

The man brought the check close to his face and studied her signature. "Mapes? You must belong to the Mapes place."

It was odd, someone looking at it that way, as if a person belonged to a place instead of the place belonging to the person. She supposed in a small community like this, with seasonal crowds coming and going, that point of view made sense.

The man closed his book with his finger holding his place. "I knew Augustus Mapes. He was a fine man."

"My grandfather."

"A real gentleman. You back for a while?"

"I'm here on vacation. Just two weeks."

"That's a shame. Well, enjoy yourself."

She put the wine in the passenger seat, backed out, and drove up Main Street. She passed a white-shingled cottage with green shutters and a sign over the door, Lake Placid Public Library. She impulsively pulled over and parked. Maybe she could find out more about Kathleen's agoraphobia and get some clues about how to encourage her to meet with the police. She didn't seem to be able to leave the desperate look in those green eyes behind and simply enjoy her time off.

She glanced at the wine and decided not to worry about someone stealing it. Not in small-town USA.

The middle-aged woman sitting on a high stool behind a tall oak desk could have answered a casting call for village librarian. "May I help you?"

August looked around the warm room. There was a stone fireplace on one wall and four rocking chairs lining the windows facing the lake. Not the kind of library likely to carry much material about phobias. "I'm looking for information about psychological conditions."

"What a nice coincidence. We just received a new book. It's in the reference section on the left." The librarian climbed down from her stool and led the way. She looked back over her shoulder. "You'll be the first to read the book. I just completed cataloguing it in with a Dewey Decimal number. I suspect you're not local. Did you know Melvil Dewey was a longtime resident of our town?"

August smiled. The librarian enjoyed having someone to talk to. Librarian in Lake Placid, New York was probably a pretty solitary job. She held out her hand. "I'm August Mapes."

"Lily Webster." She ran her finger along the spines of several books. "Yes, here it is." She pulled the heavy book off the shelf and put it in August's hands as though presenting a prize.

August read aloud the title imprinted in gold letters on the front cover. "Diagnostic and Statistical Manual of Mental Disorders. This might be just what I'm looking for."

The librarian nodded. She beamed with personal pride at satisfying August's request. "I'm afraid you can't check the book out. It's for reference only."

"That will do fine. Mrs. Webster, may I borrow some paper and a pencil?"

"Certainly, dear."

August took the book and sat in one of the rocking chairs. The windows overlooked a canopy of brightly colored leaves marching down to the lake and the sun sparkled off a light chop on the water's surface. She thought about the irony of the moment. In the presence of this beauty, she was preparing to read about Kathleen's condition from a catalogue of human misery. She turned to the index and found *Agoraphobia; see also anxiety disorders; panic attacks*. The indicated entry confirmed the way Kathleen described her disability.

Agoraphobics are afraid of having a panic attack in public. They avoid situations they perceive to be beyond their control. Kathleen said she couldn't tolerate riding elevators, standing in lines, driving over bridges and through tunnels, or taking public transportation.

The condition can be caused by a history of very stressful or traumatic events. The car accident that killed her parents would certainly qualify, but Kathleen said she didn't remember anything about the crash or her time in the hospital. It could be that she suppressed the memories. Had she experienced other traumatic events?

At its most severe, sufferers become homebound. In less severe cases, the patient sets up a habitual routine and/or recruits a trusted helper.

How severe had Kathleen's condition become? She told August she was able to go to some familiar places. She certainly appeared to be recruiting August as a trusted helper.

The end of the entry talked about treatment.

Medication and psychotherapy, combined with gentle exposure to the object of their fears, are the most effective intervention.

Was Kathleen under the care of a psychiatrist? How could August assure a police interview would be "gentle"?

She brought the heavy volume back to the librarian, thanked her, and returned to her car. Sure enough, the wine was still in the passenger seat. She took the road skirting the lake's shore toward the cabin. Two miles along, her boathouse came into view. Lucas Grigsby, handyman, gardener, and all-around caretaker for the cabin, was setting out gleaming white Adirondack chairs on the deck next to the boat slips. She beeped the horn twice and braked next to the deck. "Hi, Mr. Grigsby."

He took off his hat and wiped his forehead with his sleeve. He eyed the Austin-Healey. "I'm glad to see you made the trip safe, Miss August." Lucas was the kind of old-time Yankee who didn't trust speedy little foreign sports cars. "Millie is up in the kitchen. She's got some lunch fixed for you."

"Thanks, Mr. Grigsby. If you have time, will you bring down the canoe?"

"Sure thing. Going for a paddle?"

"I might."

"You be careful now, Miss August."

She waved at him and turned right onto the winding drive leading up to the rambling brown-shingled house. Her family had always called the house 'the cabin,' but it was far from a one-room log structure the word suggested. The house was grand in a rustic sort of way. Her grandfather built it in 1910, big and comfortable enough to accommodate his family and their friends as a summer getaway from the city. The main house with its outbuildings sat on two acres of woods overlooking the lake. August's father inherited the property from her grandfather, and upon her father's death, the property passed to her.

She pulled out her suitcase and the wine and raised the top on her car. She heard the screen door slam. A short, stout, grey-haired woman came down the stairs, wiping her hands on her apron.

"Miss August."

August hugged the woman. "It's good to see you, Millie."

Millie took the suitcase. "Let me help with your case. I've made up the corner bedroom for you. It's always been your favorite, with the best view of the lake." She led the way through the kitchen into the large great room.

August stopped in the middle of the room and turned in a circle. "I need just a second to take in this wonderful space. I forget between times how special this room is." The quartersawn oak floors shone with a golden glow. The ceiling rose twenty feet to exposed beams. Across the wall facing the lake, floor-to-ceiling windows let in the natural light. A huge fieldstone fireplace covered the opposite wall. Furnishings she remembered from her earliest years filled the room: brown leather chairs in front of the fireplace, matching Tiffany lamps on end tables, elk antlers above the mantel, a bookcase filled with paperbacks, jigsaw puzzles, and board games.

Millie gestured toward the fireplace. "Lucas laid you a fire in case you want one. Evenings are getting chilly already."

They went up the stairs to the end of the hallway. The bedroom was on a corner with a view of the lake to the west and evergreen forest to the south. Millie placed August's suitcase on the foot of the bed. "You get settled, and then I have some lunch fixed."

August hugged the woman again. "Millie, you and Mr. Grigsby are the best. The place looks wonderful."

Millie smiled. "You still call him 'Mr. Grigsby.'"

"My grandfather insisted on my showing him respect, and old habits die hard."

Millie whispered behind her hand. "He likes it."

Chapter Three

THAT EVENING, AUGUST MADE herself breakfast for supper, her favorite, and took her wine out to the sleeping porch to watch the sun set over the lake. She heard the steady *thwack-thwack* of a neighbor chopping firewood. Practical work, and a great way to stay in shape. She resolved to wake up early for a run. If she did that every morning, she could go back to New York not just mentally rested but also feeling physically restored.

The sun dropping below the western horizon painted the sky with orange, purple, and amber watercolors. An owl called to his mate from one of the tall white pines by the lake. She looked at the empty lounge chair beside her and remembered an evening much like this five years before. June had sat in the chair, sipping wine. They had come to the cabin for a getaway from insanely busy work schedules, hoping to resurrect their relationship.

They had met in law school. August and June were the only women in their class at Columbia. Their contracts professor made a lame joke the first day about both of them being named for months of the year. They avoided each other for weeks, each trying to establish her own identity. They were careful to find seats on opposite sides of the lecture hall. But they couldn't help catching each other's eyes when professors and classmates referred to them as 'the girls.' August hid a satisfied smile when professors called on June with a particularly thorny hypothetical and June nailed the answer.

One night, August braved freezing rain to study in Butler Library. As she climbed the stone steps, slick with ice, she slipped and fell backward into June's arms.

"Careful." June kept a steadying hand on the small of August's back till they got to the top of the stairs and inside the front door.

August stamped the water from her boots. "Thanks. How embarrassing."

June shrugged. "It happens." She stuck her hand out. "June Fleming."

"I know." August took her hand. "August Mapes."

"I know. Do you think we might stop dodging each other?"

August nodded. "We might even help each other. I admire your grasp of real estate law. Some days Professor Morris might as well be speaking in tongues."

"And you appear to know your way around contracts, where I could certainly use some help." They sat together in the library that night and left together around midnight. June stopped on the sidewalk under a streetlight. "Come to my apartment Sunday for dinner, and we'll make each other even smarter."

They began studying together every weekend. One Saturday night in June's apartment they sat cross-legged on pillows at the coffee table, eating Chinese takeout and drinking wine and arguing about what would constitute an unenforceable contract. June had soft jazz playing on the radio. She emptied the last of the wine into August's glass.

"Are you trying to get me drunk?"

"It's the only way I can win this argument."

In the background, "Moonglow" began with a clarinet flourish. June said, "I love this song." She stood and took August's hand and pulled her to her feet. They embraced easily and naturally. In their sock feet, they were the same height. They swayed in time to the music. June hummed the tune in August's ear. Her warm breath sent chills down August's back. June kissed her neck and pulled away to look into her eyes. "Do you mind?"

August shook her head. To show her, she took June's face in her hands and kissed her on the mouth. Her lips tasted of the wine, like cinnamon and pepper. She held the kiss while they sank to their knees. June pulled the pillows over, and they lay facing each other. August unbuttoned June's blouse halfway down and pulled it over her head. She hesitated. She had felt crushes for

28

girls as far back as she could remember, but her lovemaking had been in fantasies. This was a real woman's body under her hands.

June sensed her uncertainty. "Okay, this is your first time."

August nodded.

June gently pushed her onto her back. "Let me show you."

***

Within a few weeks, August had moved in with June. They finished law school in the top ten percent of their class, and a prestigious New York law firm, Hampton, Garrick, and Liszt, picked both of them for internships while they studied for the bar exam.

The Japanese bombed Pearl Harbor, and young men lined up to enlist in the war, causing a shortage of young attorneys. Bad news for the country was good news for the two women. HGL hired them full time, June in the tax division and August in corporate mergers and acquisitions. They worked eighty-hour weeks, and their physical relationship, which had started red-hot, began to suffer. There never seemed to be time for intimacy. Almost without either of them noticing, they drifted apart. It wasn't another person or money problems or a clash of values that came between them, it was their ambition and work ethic.

The women had worked three years at HGL when the war ended and young male lawyers came marching home. The men began getting plum assignments and partnership offers. August decided to leave the big law firm and start her own practice. She bought the brownstone on Washington Square North for her office on the first floor and moved into an apartment upstairs. She and June managed to stay friends through the breakup. They kept in touch, mostly by phone and less frequently as time went on. They both had flings here and there, exalted with each other at the exciting beginnings and cried on each other's shoulders when they ended.

August's practice struggled for the first few months. At least half of her prospective clients were shocked to find she was a woman. Some turned and walked out. She developed the attitude of "Their Loss" and moved on. Over time, through word of mouth and because of her competence, she developed a reputation for compassionate representation of women divorcing their husbands and relentless pursuit of fairness for them.

The owl called again, louder and more insistent. She drained her wineglass. Maybe she should call June to see if she could add any pieces to the Kathleen O'Brien puzzle. She went downstairs to the phone and dialed the direct line to June's desk at the law firm in New York. June picked up on the first ring. "Fleming."

"June, it's August. I'd say I'm surprised to find you still at your desk, but I'm not. Have the old boys wised up about offering you a partnership yet?"

"Hold on a minute." August heard June's office door close. "No partnership offer yet. I just go ahead being the biggest biller in the tax department and trust my day will come. I know that's one of the main reasons you left, because they've got an aversion to partners without male appendages."

"That, certainly, but my reason for leaving was more I felt I was simply assisting wealthy companies get wealthier. I wanted the feeling of helping people more directly, as individuals."

"That's exactly why I sent Kathleen O'Brien to you. You're calling me about her case, right? Sounds like she could use some special individual help."

August wanted to be careful to avoid disclosing confidential information. "How much did Kathleen O'Brien tell you about her situation?"

"Enough to know the matter is outside my bailiwick. I stick to numbers and the tax code. Much less complicated than people problems."

"How did she come to you in the first place?"

"I knew her family growing up in New Canaan. I used to babysit Kathleen, and I had a huge crush on the mother, Francine. She was wonderful. I was obsessed with her for a whole year."

"That's funny. Kathleen says she had a crush on you."

"Nonsense. She was a child, six or seven. I was thirteen or fourteen. I assume she told you about her parents being killed.

What a tragedy that was. I guess she doesn't know any other lawyers to advise her about the matter at hand, so she called me. I thought of you because you've told me you have access to a good investigator who's a former police detective."

"Yes, Blackie is great. Do you know anything about Kathleen's life after her parents were killed?"

"I think there was an aunt and uncle, the mother's brother and sister. The aunt lived in the city. That's all I know. Before she contacted me, I haven't heard from Kathleen, or anything about her, since the accident."

June wouldn't be able to answer her questions about other traumatic events in Kathleen's life or the extent of her agoraphobia.

"Hey, you were chiding me about working late. What about you? You're still working tonight."

August looked out the window at lights winking on Buck Island in the middle of the lake. "As a matter of fact, I'm in Lake Placid."

"Oh. Lucky you." June was silent a moment. "Do you remember when we were there five years ago?"

"Of course."

"Do you remember it fondly?"

August laughed. "Of course. I was just thinking about that time."

"I remember too. That bedroom with the view of the lake. I'll bet you're sitting on the sleeping porch drinking wine."

"I am."

"Wish I was there too. When you're back in town we should get together. The firm has courtside seats for the Knicks. We could go to the season opener. Or maybe you prefer the Philharmonic. We have orchestra seats. I remember your theory about lesbians, that we fall into one of two buckets, jock lesbians or arty lesbians."

"Don't remind me what a naïve know-it-all I used to be."

June chuckled. "Part of your charm."

"Thanks. Well, I'll let you get back to your billable hours."

"Seriously, call me to get together. And let me know if I can help with Kathleen O'Brien—anything to do with numbers or the tax code, that is."

Chapter Four

BLACKIE RYE, PRIVATE DETECTIVE, took the chair across the desk in August's office. He adjusted his tweed jacket and straightened his maroon knit tie. "Wonderful to see you again, Miss Mapes."

August smiled. "And you, Mr. Rye." Before meeting Blackie in person four years before, she had a picture of what a retired NYPD detective would look like. She couldn't have been more wrong in Blackie's case. He looked and sounded more like an academic than an ex-cop. His grey hair curled over his shirt collar, and he wore reading glasses perched on the tip of his nose. He had confessed to her that before he retired, his nickname in the squad room was "The Professor."

He pulled a small notebook from the inside pocket of his jacket. "The identity of our author remains a mystery. First, the name, E. Gamin. Ambiguous as to gender and ethnicity. There are no Gamins in the Ridgewood or New Canaan phone directories and only six in Manhattan, none with the first initial E. No surprise to discover he or she is probably using an alias. Especially since E. Gamin is an anagram for 'enigma.'

"Next, fingerprints. I've got a friend from the old days who still works in forensics. I caught him in his last week before retirement. He went over the envelopes and their contents. There are three sets of prints. Yours and Lena's show up in the Department of Motor Vehicles database. I'm thinking the third set are your client's, but Sam couldn't come up with a match for her in any of his databases."

"Not a surprise. She rarely leaves her apartment, and I suspect she doesn't drive."

"E. Gamin likely wore gloves, hence no prints belonging to him."

He flipped a page in the notebook. "Then I tried tracking down the PO boxes. Renting these things anonymously is easy.

You can write William Shakespeare on the rental form and pay in cash and nobody asks any questions. I visited both boxes. They were empty. Same thing with the money orders. To trace one, you have to be in possession of a receipt number only the purchaser has."

"Will E. Gamin know when and if Miss O'Brien cashes the money order?"

"He will if he bothers to check with Western Union."

He consulted his notes again. "I made a trip to New Canaan to follow up on the details about the car accident. Small town like that, you can pick up a lot just by asking a few leading questions and being a good listener. I spent a half day drinking coffee in the diner on Main Street. I learned the whole town was stunned by the tragedy. The O'Briens and the teenagers in the other car were all well-known in town. The O'Brien family was active in the community and their church. The parents didn't make it to the hospital alive. Some precious time elapsed between the collision and help arriving because the driver fled the scene. It was late at night, and the accident went unreported for a half hour. The parents died in the ambulance on the way to the hospital. The little girl survived with relatively minor injuries.

"About the teenagers. The driver, David Gates, was a smart kid, a leader in his class, all set to go to Harvard. He and his girlfriend in the front seat were miraculously uninjured. In the back seat the passengers were another boy and girl. Sarah Franks, homecoming queen, died on the scene of a broken neck. The impact threw her into the back of the front seat. Her boyfriend was captain of the football team. He was to start Yale in the fall on a full football scholarship. He suffered two broken legs and spent six months in the hospital."

August shook her head. "Tragic all the way around."

"Yes."

August flipped the page of her yellow legal tablet. "When do you think we should go to the police? I'm concerned about my client's safety. The killer, if it was a murder, knows where she lives."

Blackie shook his head. "I suspect NYPD Homicide would find what we have so far pretty thin, especially since the death is outside their jurisdiction. The New Canaan police are apparently buying Gates's death as a suicide."

August tapped a cadence on her desk with a pencil. "You're saying it's a dead end."

"So far, but there may be more clues in the story itself."

"Like what?"

"Like the etorphine hydrochloride injection the killer used on the victim. You don't just go into a pharmacy and buy that drug off the shelf. Maybe I can find out if he actually bought it and didn't just make it up for the story. Another lead might be the football player. He's still in town." He checked his notes. "Carl Tobias. He runs a diner with his mother. I'd like a chance to talk to him. He might hold a grudge against David Gates. Maybe enough to kill him."

"I assumed the author is in New York City. The PO boxes are all in Manhattan."

"Tobias would be unlikely to rent a box in New Canaan, if he's E. Gamin. Too easy to track him there."

August nodded. "I'd like to be in on your interview with him."

"Good. I was thinking of going back to New Canaan tomorrow."

"That works for me. I'll drive. Meet me here at ten. We can be at Tobias's diner by eleven."

Blackie rose and headed for the door. She stopped him. "And Blackie, while you're at it, see what you can find out about Kathleen O'Brien."

August followed him out and stopped at Lena's desk. "Get Miss O'Brien on the phone, please."

Lena transferred the call to August's phone. "Hello, Kathleen."

"So, you're back from your lumberjack road trip."

"Yes." August looked down at her navy pinstriped business suit over an off-white silk blouse and smiled. She liked being teased by this attractive woman. "I can give you an update on what we've found so far."

"And I have news for you too. Can we meet in person?"

August supposed a walk across the park wouldn't be unpleasant. "I'll be there in ten minutes." She grabbed her tablet and pencil and waved at Lena as she started out the front door. "Back in an hour or so."

"Now shall I start a client file? We're beginning to rack up costs, you know."

August tapped her finger on her lips. "Yes, I guess we should."

She jaywalked across Washington Square North and passed under the arch into the park. During the two weeks of her Lake Placid vacation, New York had left summer behind and moved into full-on autumn, her favorite time of year in the city. The sun was bright but couldn't quite heat up the chilly breeze sweeping newspapers and red and burnt umber leaves across her path. The children around the fountain were the younger siblings of the school-aged boys and girls one saw in the summertime. The park was quieter without the high-pitched squeals of the older kids.

She pushed the apartment's buzzer, and Kathleen came to meet her at the front door. She wore a simple linen dress again, this time burnt umber, exactly the color of the leaves in the park and a match for her hair. She embraced August. "I'm so glad to see you." She took August's hand and led her up the stairs and into the apartment and drew her down on the couch. "Shall I give you my news first?"

August nodded.

"Just as you said, I edited the chapter about the drunk driver and sent it back to the Penn Station post office box. I made some suggestions about adding more detail to close some of the gaps in the timeline and plot. I thought we might get the author to give more clues to his identity."

"Smart."

"He's already sent his second draft back to me. Here it is." She handed August another manila envelope. "This envelope is just like the first two, except the return address on this one is a box at the post office in the financial district."

"You haven't opened it."

"I waited for you. I wasn't sure what to do."

"Open it. See what changes he made."

Kathleen tore the envelope open. "Here's a note." She read it aloud.

My dear Miss O'Brien,

I am so happy you reconsidered taking on my project. I trust my sending the newspaper articles about the tragic accident and the death of the driver weren't too disturbing for you. I was simply anxious for you to understand that you and I will work together unusually well, being on the same wavelength.

Your suggestions for improving the story are very helpful. I hope you'll find I've followed them to the letter. I'm using your suggestions about the first story to improve a second chapter, which I'll be sending shortly.

I'm looking forward to our next communication.
Very truly yours,
E. Gamin

Kathleen read silently through the story. "He made the corrections I suggested."

"You read the whole thing that fast?"

She shrugged. "I'm an editor. It's what I do. Just a minute." She went to the desk for a blue pencil to mark the changes. "He put in a scene about doing research in the *New York Times* morgue. The description is actually quite good."

August took the pages and the manila envelope. "That's helpful." She patted Kathleen's hand. "You did a good job. I'm afraid we didn't make any progress finding Mr. Gamin. It's no surprise E. Gamin is an alias. Tracing the post office boxes proved a dead end. Same with the money order. We may be able to track down some of the clues from the story, especially with the additional detail he added. We need more before involving the police."

"What should I do now?"

"If this were a normal editing job, what would you do at this point?"

"We're done with the first chapter."

"So you write him back at the new post office box and tell him the edit is complete and see what happens next."

"What would I do without you?" Kathleen took August's hand. "Tell me about your trip."

"I spent some rejuvenating time at my family cabin in Lake Placid."

"Oh, the skiing town."

"Yes."

"Why did you need to rejuvenate?"

"Recovering from a particularly difficult case."

"What kind of a case?"

"I can't talk about it with you."

"Of course, just like you wouldn't tell anyone about my case."

"That's right. While I was in Lake Placid, I did some research on your agoraphobia. Tell me about the panic attacks."

"It's hard to describe, but I'll try. Are you aware of your heartbeats?"

August held her breath and listened. She shook her head. "No, I'm not."

"Most people aren't. I am, constantly, even in my sleep. The panic attack starts with my heart racing at ten times normal. I struggle to get air into my lungs. My body feels like I'm dying, and I'm helpless to save myself."

"Terrifying. What brings on the attack?"

"That's the awful thing. The onset doesn't seem to be related to anything happening around me. It's not as though something triggers my anxiety and my body reacts. If that were the case, I could avoid those things. Instead, the panic attack comes out of the blue. As long as I stay in a safe place, I feel in control, able to get help if I need it unexpectedly."

August looked around the pleasant apartment. "I can see how you'd feel safe here. Apparently, there are other things someone suffering with the condition can do too, medication and therapy. Have you ever tried seeing someone, like a psychiatrist?"

A shadow passed across Kathleen's face. She shook her head. "I tried that a long time ago. The therapy didn't go well." She gazed into August's eyes. "I feel very safe with you." She held August's right hand palm-down under her left breast. "See? My heart is normal now."

August marveled at how Kathleen's breast felt soft and firm at the same time. In the silence, the ticking of the grandfather clock in the corner matched the beats of Kathleen's heart. Kathleen held August's hand hard against her chest and whispered, "Do you feel it?"

August swallowed and nodded. Kathleen leaned close and kissed her lightly on the lips. Her hair brushed August's cheek. It smelled of a mix of spice and some flower, maybe hyacinth. August pulled her hand back and moved away.

"Kathleen, you're very attractive, but as long as you're my client, it's best we keep things on a professional basis."

"I've made you uncomfortable. I understand. It's some sort of ethical regulation, like a priest or a therapist."

"Not exactly, but I have my own rules. In my experience, sticking to the policy just keeps things simpler." She picked up her legal tablet. "Let's make a plan for where we go next."

Jane Alden

Chapter Five

PEGGY'S DINER SAT ON the outskirts of New Canaan, where banks, dress shops, and department stores gave way to gas stations, used car lots, and secondhand furniture stores. Gravel crunched under the tires of August's sports car as she and Blackie pulled into a space near the diner's entrance. The lot was almost empty. Above the front door, a neon sign buzzed, the capital *P* blinking on and off.

August killed the engine. "You take the lead in the questioning. I suspect you'll be able to get more out of him."

Blackie nodded.

A few men occupied stools at the chrome counter. August and Blackie slid into a red booth across from the blackboard advertising the day's special, meatloaf and mashed potatoes. The air smelled of a mix of recycled grease and coffee. An elderly woman in a pink waitress uniform approached them with two thick coffee mugs in one hand and a pot in the other.

"Coffee?"

They said yes in unison.

The waitress poured their coffee. "What'll you have to eat?" She gestured with the coffee pot. "Special's up there on the board."

August and Blackie said just coffee in unison.

The waitress shrugged. "Suit yourself."

Blackie cleared his throat. "Is Mr. Tobias here?"

The waitress put her hand on her hip. "Depends."

"On what?"

"Whether you mean Carl Senior or Carl Junior. Carl Senior is dead." She nodded toward the kitchen. "If you mean Carl Junior, he's in the back."

Blackie handed her a business card. "Can you ask Carl Junior if we might have a few words?"

After a minute, Carl Tobias pushed through the swinging door. He paused to take off his apron and look August and Blackie over. His white cotton T-shirt stretched taut across his heavily muscled chest and arms. He picked up a cane from underneath the counter and limped over to their booth. "What can I do for you?"

"Mr. Tobias, I'm Blackie Rye and this is August Mapes. We are representing Kathleen O'Brien in a business matter. I imagine Miss O'Brien's name is familiar to you."

Tobias lowered himself into the booth next to Blackie. He caught the waitress's eye and mimed a cup of coffee for himself. "She's the little girl in the car we hit."

"That's right. So you've kept up with her?"

"No, but I'm not likely to have forgotten her name, am I?" He shifted in his seat and rubbed his knee. "What sort of a business matter can I help you with?"

"Miss O'Brien is a book editor. She's considering taking on an assignment that may relate to your accident twenty years ago."

The waitress set a full mug in front of Tobias. He spooned three scoops of sugar into the coffee and took his time answering while he stirred. "I'd say you're better off talking to David Gates, but it's a little late for that."

"So you know about his death?"

"Yes, I know he killed himself. New Canaan is a small town. Thing like that causes a stir."

"Did you and Mr. Gates stay in touch after the accident?"

"Nah. He got out of jail about the same time I got out of the hospital, but we went separate ways. I'd see him around some, at a high school football game or more often in a bar."

"You've stayed here in New Canaan."

Tobias looked around the diner and smirked. "Where else would I go? I took over the diner when my dad died. My mom couldn't run the place by herself, and I had limited options." He tapped his right leg with the cane. "This wasn't the plan, but what do they say? 'Life is what happens while you're making other plans.'"

Blackie nodded. "You were set to start Yale on a football scholarship."

"The wreck put an end to that. I won't be on a football field again. Not until I have my ashes scattered on the fifty-yard line."

August looked into his face for a sign he was making a dark joke. He wasn't. "David Gates changed your life, along with a lot of others, by getting behind the wheel drunk." She waited for some indication that Tobias held a grudge.

Tobias rubbed the back of his hand across his mouth. "What is it you're here for?"

"Mr. Tobias, can you think of anyone who would be holding a grudge against Mr. Gates?"

"Are you implying he didn't kill himself? From what I've heard around town, he had plenty of reasons to think the world might be better off without him. If you're asking if I had something to do with his death, the answer is no. I've put the past behind me. Moved on. I've got enough to worry about without plotting some kind of revenge." He shook his head. "No."

August held out her hand. "We're doing our due diligence in order to advise Miss O'Brien, and you've been generous with your time. Thank you, Mr. Tobias."

Tobias shook her hand and stood up. "Just tell her I wish her the best."

Blackie paid for their coffees with a generous tip, and they headed the car back toward the center of town.

August glanced across at Blackie. "What do you think? Could he be E. Gamin?"

Blackie shrugged. "Hard to say. As a killer, he wouldn't be very fast on his feet, but he'd make up for his disability with upper body strength. He denies any bad blood between him and Gates. It's not clear to me how he'd have access to the drug the killer used to knock out his victim in the story. We didn't probe that with him."

Blackie took out his notebook and made some entries. "How about we stop by the police station since we're here? It's on our way."

"I'll drop you off. You and the boys can talk cop to cop. I'll drive by Gates's house. You've got the address in your book, right?"

She found the house on Mulberry Road. It looked as described in the story, a Norman Tudor with an attached garage on the left. There was a For Sale sign in the front yard. She pulled to the curb in front of the house across the street and looked around. This was the very spot the killer in the story sat scoping out his prey. A neighbor in a straw hat and gardening gloves trimmed roses along a picket fence. August suspected she might be the anonymous source quoted in the newspaper account of Gates's death. She got out of the car and waved to the woman. "Hello. That's a charming place for sale across the street. Do you think the lady of the house would mind if I rang the doorbell?"

The woman eyed August's Austin-Healey and expensive suit. "Oh, the place is empty, dear. Mrs. Gates, the lady of the house, moved back to Michigan months ago. Call the realtor. The number's on the sign there. Are you relocating to our fair town?"

She reminded August of a bright-eyed, curious little bird. "I'm considering it. This seems like a nice, quiet neighborhood."

The woman gazed for a moment at the garage across the street. "It always had been until recently."

"Oh?"

The woman went back to clipping her roses. "I'll just say we're all looking forward to new owners."

August headed to her car. "I'll let you get back to your beautiful flowers. Thank you."

The woman waved. "Call the realtor."

Blackie was waiting outside the police headquarters. "I talked to the chief. Gates had multiple DWIs, the last one a few months ago. He was set to go to court, probably going to jail. He died a week before the court date."

"The impending court date might account for the timing of the murder, if it was a murder."

"It could also account for the timing of a suicide." Blackie consulted his notes. "The police didn't dust for prints on the hose

44

or tape. It's a small police department without forensics capability, and the chief made a judgement call against spending the money for outside help. No autopsy. The body was cremated, and the remains are unclaimed at the local funeral home. There's no question in the chief's mind the death was suicide."

"Good work, Blackie. I found Gates's house. It looks just like the one portrayed in the story. It's for sale. The neighbor lady said the wife left months ago. She could have gotten sick of bailing him out. The most recent arrest may have been the last straw for her, and if his death was suicide, her leaving might have pushed him over the edge."

They passed a sprawling group of identical small white bungalows. Blackie pointed out the car's side window. "That housing development reminds me. You asked me to see what I could find out about Kathleen O'Brien. Her father was a successful residential real estate developer. He specialized in affordable bungalows in the suburbs. When the Depression began easing, things really took off for his construction company. The development we just passed could be one of his."

"So he must have left Miss O'Brien well off financially?"

"Very. She has a healthy bank account. Shall I give you the rest of it?"

She nodded.

"You know about the car accident that killed her parents. She had no siblings. The only remaining family are an aunt and uncle, Louis and Carole Collins. Brother and sister of the mother. They became her guardians after the accident. She went to a couple of boarding schools in Manhattan and then to Barnard for a BA. She got a manuscript reader's job right out of college at Summit Press. Five years ago, she left the publisher and became a freelance editor. She must love the work because, as I said, she doesn't need the money. No arrests. Not even a jaywalking ticket."

They rode in silence for a while. "What about the aunt and uncle? They could hold a grudge against Gates. I'd like to talk with both of them. Call Lena with their contact information and I'll get working on appointments with them. And start thinking about the best way to get NYPD involved. I'm anxious to get this in their hands."

Blackie made some notes in his little book and put it back in his pocket. "One question nags at me. What would make someone connected to an accident twenty years ago angry enough to kill Gates now?"

"You said he was still risking lives by driving drunk. Maybe someone wanted to stop him before he caused another tragedy." She glanced at Blackie. "Are you thinking what I'm thinking? If you and I weren't terminally suspicious, we might agree with the New Canaan police chief about Gates's death being a suicide. Maybe it's just a story. Maybe E. Gamin saw the newspaper article and took the facts and wove a tale out of them."

"Maybe." They said it in unison.

Chapter Six

AUGUST WAS TAKING ADVANTAGE of the first full day she'd had in her office since accepting Kathleen O'Brien as a client. She and Lena worked all morning catching up on outstanding cases, and the afternoon was back-to-back appointments with new clients.

The middle-aged woman across the desk from August blew her nose and dabbed at her eyes again.

August came around the desk and patted her shoulder. "You leave this up to me, Mrs. Thompson. I'll work on the issues we've discussed and my secretary will arrange our next appointment in about two weeks." She walked the woman past Lena's desk to the front door. Her last client of the day sat in the waiting area, patiently flipping through a magazine. The phone on Lena's desk rang.

"Law offices. How may I help you?" Lena listened for a moment then put her hand over the receiver and mouthed, "Kathleen O'Brien."

August took the call in her office. "Kathleen, may I call you back later this evening? We're snowed under right now."

"I got another chapter. He left me a story about another murder." Kathleen's voice was breathless as though she had run a long way.

"What do you mean he left you a story?"

"I heard a rustling noise in the hallway outside my apartment. I waited a while because I was too scared to open the door. When I did get up enough courage to peek out, he was gone, and there was a manila envelope leaning against the doorjamb. It's just like the others except this one has no postmark. He delivered it to my front door. Maybe I can meet you halfway in the park."

"You stay right where you are. Keep the door locked and don't open it for anyone. I have one more appointment and then I'll come to you."

***

It was dark when August finished her last appointment. The woman told a story so familiar it sounded like a cliché. Her husband of twenty-five years bought a red Jaguar sports car, began wearing briefs instead of boxers, and announced one evening at the dinner table that he was leaving her for his twenty-year-old secretary.

Lena saw the woman out, handing her a few tissues to go.

"Go home, Lena. It's late."

"Are you going to Miss O'Brien's?"

"Yes."

"I'll walk with you across the park."

"I'll be fine. Go home."

August decided to take MacDougal Street, bordering the park on the west, instead of cutting through. It was better lighted, and she expected there would be more people about, but it turned out the area was deserted. A mist hung over the street. Footsteps on the cobblestones echoed off the buildings. Were they her own, or was someone matching her step for step? She stopped and looked behind her. No one. She shook her head and smiled. E. Gamin's story was getting to her.

Kathleen buzzed August in and met her at the front door of the apartment. She handed August a manila envelope with Kathleen's name written on the front in the familiar block-printed letters. August sat on the sofa and shook out the typed pages.

My dear Kathleen,

I hope I haven't overstepped by hand-delivering my second chapter to your apartment door. I'm quite anxious to know what you think of the enclosed priest story. I've looked back over your comments from the first chapter to make sure to avoid repeating past mistakes in this one. As the expert you are, you'd find it amusing how carefully I ponder each word before typing it. I'm reminded of a quote from Oscar Wilde, "I was working on the

*proof of one of my poems all the morning and took out a comma.
In the afternoon I put it back again."*

*Anxiously awaiting your response,
E. Gamin*

August laid the note aside. "He's gone from calling you Miss
O'Brien to Kathleen and coming to your door. This is very
unsettling. We need to bring the police in as soon as possible."
She read on.

Father Alphonse

*I stood in the misty rain on the corner across from the park.
Taxis swished by on Fifth Avenue. The nineteenth-century granite
mansions lining the street appeared to have risen organically from
the ground rather than to have been built by mortals. I read the
motto chiseled over the heavy wooden double front doors of No.
1, East 92nd Street.* Convent of the Blessed Virgin, Empowering
Girls' Unique Potential. *A coal baron donated this stately home in
1880, to Sister Katherine Bernadette for her girls' school. She must
have been a master salesman. I imagined the pitch she made to
the cynical tycoon in his black suit and stiff white collar. "I'll
empower your granddaughters to realize their unique potential."*

*I checked my watch. 4:30. I crossed the street, climbed the
wide stone steps, and pulled open the heavy front door. The
marble foyer floor gleamed. A curving staircase rose to the second
floor. A nun with her arms full of books came from a door on the
left. "May I help you?"*

"I want to talk with someone about my niece."

"Is she one of our students?"

"Not yet. That's what I'd like to speak with someone about."

*"Just a moment, please." She went back in the door. After a
minute or two, she came into the foyer again, this time without
the books. "Come this way, please." She held the door open.*

Inside, there was a high counter and across the room a door with a nameplate: Mother Marie Madeline, Headmistress.

"This way."

The nun knocked lightly and opened the door. The headmistress stood and smiled. Should I shake hands with the headmistress or bow or what? I stuck out my hand. "Chris Roper."

She took my hand with the grip of a steamfitter. "Sister Teresa said you're here about your niece?" She gestured toward the visitor chair.

"Yes. My niece is nine years old. Her parents were tragically killed in a car accident and I am her legal guardian."

Mother Marie Madeline made the sign of the cross. "God rest their souls."

"Yes, well, I'm familiar with your school's wonderful reputation. I was hoping for a tour and information about how she might be considered for admission."

"Certainly." She opened a drawer in a file cabinet behind her and took out a folder. "You'll find information about our school, our history, mission, faculty, and educational offerings. Your niece, at her age, would be in our lower school."

I pulled out the insert with color photographs of two dozen or so faculty and staff. At the top, Mother Marie Madeline, and under her picture...there he was. Father Alphonse. He was in his mid-sixties, with a receding hairline and pale blue, rheumy eyes. Across his nose and cheeks, broken capillaries told a tale of sustained alcohol abuse. Not a surprise. Drinking helped him live with what he'd done.

Mother Marie Madeline checked her watch. "I can give you a quick look now. You may want to bring your niece in for a more extensive tour and an interview when we have more time. We like to be sure the Convent is going to be a good fit for our prospective students." She led the way to the foyer. "The basement and first floor are administration and support services; kitchen and dining hall, housekeeping, and so on. At this time of the day, the girls are in their second-floor rooms, studying and preparing for vespers and the evening meal."

We took the stairs to the third floor and looked in on empty classrooms smelling of chalk dust and wet wool. "The top floor houses the chapel and ballroom. We're very proud of our fine arts program. We have orchestra, dance, art, and drama. Our girls are very well-rounded." A bell's tolling above our heads interrupted her sales pitch. She looked at her watch again. "There's Father Alphonse calling us to five o'clock vespers. He's right on time, as usual."

"He tolls the bell every day?"

"Oh, yes. The vespers bell is quite the tradition. I'm a relative newcomer at the Convent, only five years. Father Alphonse has been with us for thirty years."

The vespers bell would be the key to my Phase III. Tomorrow could be the day.

Mother Marie Madeline bent to pick up a scrap of paper and tossed it in the trash. "You are welcome to join us for vespers. Our entire student body and faculty will be there. It's a good opportunity to see firsthand how we emphasize the spiritual development of our students."

"Thank you. I will."

We joined the crowd of students on the stairs headed up to the chapel. Each girl dropped a curtsy to the headmistress which she acknowledged with a nod. Some of them gave me a curious once-over. I made a mental note to be extra careful to avoid being seen by any of the girls when I returned the next day for Phase III.

In the chapel, rows of pews faced an elaborately carved pulpit. On the wall behind, a large portrait of the school's founder, Sister Katherine Bernadette, stared benevolently out at the congregation. A gilt cross hung above the painting.

Mother Marie Madeline and I took seats in the front row with the faculty. Behind us, girls in black and white Convent uniforms began filling the pews, the youngest in the front. The little girls wiggled in their seats, chattering together. In the back of the chapel, teenagers whispered to each other behind their hands.

On cue, Father Alphonse dressed in white vestments slowly descended an iron spiral staircase in the corner.

I leaned to the headmistress. "Quite dramatic. Is that the bell tower he's climbing down from?"

She nodded, and I thought I detected an eye-roll suggesting she might not be such a fan of Father Alphonse's officiousness.

The priest mounted two steps to the pulpit. He tented his fingers and gazed piously around the chapel, waiting for the girls to settle. He opened his bible and lifted his hands toward heaven. "Let us pray." A phony saint. After a half hour of prayers and bible reading, he recited a benediction, and the girls filed out of the chapel.

The headmistress walked me down the stairs and to the front entrance. "I hope you are favorably impressed with us. You can see we put an emphasis on developing our girls' lives so that all our graduates are well-rounded."

"I appreciate the short-notice tour. My family and I will talk things over."

Back out on 92nd Street, it had begun raining harder. I turned up my collar and circled the building to the freight entrance. The loading dock was deserted. I tried the door and found it unlocked. A wide hallway echoed sounds from the kitchen staff preparing to serve the evening meal. A door to the left led to back stairs. In the coal baron's day they gave the servants access to the upper floors.

I climbed to the fourth-floor landing. The door opened into the chapel, next to the bell tower stairs. I slipped out. In the picture behind the pulpit, Sister Katherine Bernadette smiled her encouragement. I climbed the bell tower stairs and hesitated, listening for any sign of the priest. All was quiet. I climbed the last few steps into a cramped room. Grey, washed-out sunlight filtered into the space from a floor-to-ceiling arched window in the south wall. Dust mites danced through the beam of light. The place could use a good cleaning.

A large brass bell was bolted to the ceiling in the room's center. A thick rope, attached to the clapper, hung straight down and ended in a coil on the floor. In one corner, an upholstered recliner with the permanent imprint of the priest's body sat next to a side table with a bottle of whiskey, a glass, a pack of cigarettes, *and an ashtray. Father Alphonse's secret hideaway. He brought little girls here to molest them, and here's where he would pay for his sins.*

***

I shifted the canvas bag strap across my shoulder. The rain had persisted overnight, feeding rivulets in the gutters and sending sheets of water down the freight entrance to the school. A delivery truck was backed up to the loading dock. The driver shouldered a crate and knocked on the door. He went inside and returned for another crate. I heard indistinct talking and a loud laugh. The driver closed the truck's tailgate, drove up the ramp, and turned left on 92nd.

I crossed the loading dock, opened the door, and peeked into the hallway. It was empty. I took the back stairs two at a time to the chapel and climbed the iron spiral stairs. Father Alphonse had visited his cave since my exploration the day before. He left cigarette butts in the ashtray and his white vestments hanging on a nail beside the chair.

I put on latex gloves, unzipped my canvas bag, and took out a painter's drop cloth, my syringe case, and an envelope addressed to Mother Marie Madeline. "Dear Mother Marie Madeline, I can no longer live with my sins. I've tried to resist the dark forces driving me, but blah...blah...blah." I looked around the room. Where would Father Alphonse put a suicide note? I propped the envelope against the whiskey bottle.

I covered the whole floor with the drop cloth and unlatched the window. It was stuck from years of disuse. I wrestled with the window till it jerked open with a cracking sound. A sudden gust of wind carried rain into the room, making dark spots like spatters of blood on the drop cloth. I closed the window, leaving it slightly ajar. A combination of the room's stuffiness and the exertion of opening the window, and maybe nerves, made sweat stand out on my forehead.

I took the syringes from the case and squirted some liquid from each one as a test.

My watch said 4:15. I stepped into the shadows to wait and practice the scenario in my head, including afterward packing up my tools and making my getaway back down the stairs and out through the loading dock. Everything would go exactly to the Phase III plan. At 4:45, I heard halting steps on the iron stairs, and the top of Father Alphonse's bald head appeared. My heart thudded in my chest. Could he hear it beating? He awkwardly hefted himself into the room and stood for a moment, hands on his hips, staring at the drop cloth. I lunged and stuck the needle into his neck. He fell to the floor like a bag of rocks. A siren approached and then faded on Fifth Avenue. I listened for any noise in the chapel below. All quiet.

I gripped the drop cloth and pulled it with the priest's limp body across the floor to the window. Moving the body was easier than I expected. I opened the window fully and tied the end of the bell rope in a double knot around his neck.

Three minutes to go until the five o'clock bell-tolling to signal vespers. I lifted my hands heavenward. "For all the little girls past and present." At exactly five o'clock, I tolled the bell four times, then tipped the priest out the window. His body dropped, and he rang the bell for the last time.

August straightened the typed pages and put them in the middle of the coffee table. "How is the priest story connected to you?"

"I went to Catholic boarding school. My aunt and uncle became my guardians when my parents died, and my aunt enrolled me."

"Go on."

Her voice took on a vague, detached quality. "It wasn't at all like in the story. The priest was kind to me. He asked me about my parents. He would pet my hair." She absentmindedly tucked a lock of auburn hair behind her ear, exposing the scar at her hairline. A vein in her temple throbbed slowly and steadily. No sign of the accelerated pulse signaling the onset of a panic attack.

In her law practice, August had encountered allegations of child abuse. She sometimes used them in court as evidence to benefit her client in custody hearings. She felt empathy for the children and the aggrieved parents, but those cases were scrubbed of emotion, full of sanitized facts in abstract testimony from a witness stand. There were no real children in front of her in court. This abuse victim was sitting across from her. August pictured a little auburn-haired nine-year-old girl, confused and grieving the loss of her parents. She struggled to control the feeling of rage that the priest would take advantage of a vulnerable child. "Did he sexually abuse you?"

"Now I know that's what it was. I didn't think so then." She leaned forward. "It was only for a short time. My uncle took me out of the school."

"Because he knew about the abuse?"

"He must have, but I didn't tell him."

"How did he suspect?"

"I don't know."

"Did he report the abuse to anyone at the school or to the police?"

"I don't know about that for sure, but they would have talked to me, wouldn't they? I don't remember anything like that. His taking me out of the school caused a huge rift between my aunt and him that has lasted till today. She had been relieved to find a place for me at Our Lady of the Assumption. She was single, busy with her career, with no interest in raising a little girl. My uncle was only twenty years old and still in college. He found a different school for me, and Aunt Carole washed her hands of both of us. I have very little contact with her."

"Are you close to your uncle?"

"We are very close. He couldn't be a complete replacement for my parents, of course. He was a young man going through challenges of his own and trying to establish himself in his career. He did his best. I visited him some during summer breaks, but I mostly stayed at school. Since my panic attacks, he visits me here and sometimes we sit in the park. We keep in touch often by phone."

"So he knows about your agoraphobia?"

"Oh, yes. As I said, we're very close."

"Does he know about E. Gamin?"

Kathleen shook her head. "You're the only one." She fingered the typed pages. "If these are more than just stories, does it mean there will be another murder?"

"We need to locate this priest at Our Lady of the Assumption. Do you remember his name?"

Kathleen shook her head. "It was so long ago. Should I edit the story like the last one?"

"Yes. I'll keep the original of this chapter with the first. I'll hurry back to the office and have Lena make a copy for you, and we'll messenger it over."

Kathleen put her hand on top of August's and intertwined their fingers. "Let me thank you properly. If you were to bring the copy back instead of sending it by messenger, I could make us a nice dinner tonight. That's allowed, isn't it?"

August accepted the caress. Kathleen's hand felt warm and strong. "I suppose that's allowed. In the meantime, keep your door locked and stay inside."

"I will. Don't worry, I have a gun."

"Wait, what? How did you get a gun?"

"Uncle Louis got it for me."

"You don't want to be in a position to have to use it. Just don't open up for anyone."

August took the manila envelope and headed for the door.

Kathleen followed her and leaned against the doorjamb. "See you about seven?"

August nodded and waited until Kathleen shut the door and she heard the click of the deadbolt.

Chapter Seven

AUGUST TUCKED THE FILE with the copy Lena had made of E. Gamin's priest story under her arm and pressed the buzzer for the top floor apartment.

A tinny version of Kathleen's voice cracked through the intercom. "Can you show yourself up?" The front door buzzed open.

August checked her reflection in the window glass and smoothed her hair and unfastened the top button of her silk blouse. She told herself to get a grip on her feelings of attraction for Kathleen. She refastened the button. She took the three flights of stairs two at a time and knocked on the apartment door.

Kathleen opened the door and a swoosh of delicious smells rushed into the hallway. She pulled August into an embrace and closed the door behind them. Spotlights illuminating the kitchen area blended with the soft glow from the shop signs across Bleeker Street. Distant sounds of the tail end of rush hour traffic harmonized with soft jazz from the radio.

August held Kathleen at arms' length. She resisted the urge to test the smoothness of her porcelain cheek with a kiss and settled instead for brushing her skin with her thumbs. Kathleen's face was tinged pink from cooking or a blush. Her hair was gathered at her neck in a loose bun. A string of pearls reflected the light from the kitchen. August took a step back. "You in an apron. That's a nice sight. What's the wonderful smell?"

"Game hens stuffed with wild rice and green beans almondine, and for dessert, Grand Marnier soufflé."

"That's impressive. Don't expect me to ever reciprocate. I scramble a mean egg, and that's about the extent of my culinary skills."

"This is not about a *quid pro quo*. Isn't that what you lawyers call it? I hope to lull you into forgetting just for tonight that I'm your client. To thank you for your help."

"Then let me get this out of the way." She handed over the folder with Lena's copy of the second chapter about the bell tower hanging.

Kathleen tossed the folder on the coffee table. "No business. This is strictly pleasure."

August looked toward the kitchen. "Tell me how I can help. I can't cook, but I'm good at taking directions."

Kathleen picked up a corkscrew and a bottle of white wine. "You can open this." She stood behind August with her arms around her waist. Her breath on the back of August's neck raised goosebumps on her skin. "Here are your directions. Ready?"

August nodded.

"You grasp the neck of the bottle in your left hand gently but firmly." She guided August's hand to the bottle and covered it with her own hand. "Place the sharp tip of the corkscrew in the exact center of the cork. It's very important that you stick the tip in the middle." August felt the pressure of Kathleen's breasts and pelvis, warm against her back. She leaned into Kathleen's body. "Then you screw clockwise."

August laughed. "I think I get the procedure." She turned to face Kathleen. "But you're making it very difficult for me to focus on the execution." She eyed the wine label. "This is nice wine. You're not only a cook, but a wine connoisseur too. I'm impressed."

Kathleen went back to the stove. "I have my moments."

August opened the wine and filled two crystal glasses. She leaned with her elbows on the counter and sipped her wine, watching Kathleen prepare the rice to stuff the birds. The ping of raindrops began on the window glass.

Kathleen tested the rice and added salt. "Raise the window a little. I love the smell of fresh rain." The open window let in the swish of passing cars below. She stuffed the birds and closed the oven. "Now we wait." She untied her apron, picked up the wine bottle and her glass, and led the way to the couch.

August lagged behind, admiring the way her dress clung to her. She couldn't help picturing her body without fabric covering the curve of her low back where it flared into firm buttocks. She took a big swig of wine. She had to be honest with herself. She came to dinner knowing full well she'd face temptation to violate her own rule about becoming involved with a client. She could feel her resolve slipping.

Kathleen kicked off her shoes and sat on the couch with her legs tucked under her. She smiled and patted the couch. "Aren't you going to sit down?"

August sat and crossed her legs at the knees.

Kathleen shifted to face her directly. "You know everything about me. Tell me about you. Let's play Four Questions."

"Four Questions?"

Kathleen refilled their wineglasses. "It's a game I play with my authors to help them bring their characters to life, to make them more than merely words on the page. The four questions are: Where was your protagonist born? How many siblings does she have? What was her greatest challenge growing up? If she could change one thing about herself, what would that be?"

August relaxed a little. The game seemed safer than letting the music and the wine lead her in the wrong direction. "So you want me to answer those questions? I will, but you have to go first."

Kathleen laughed. "As I said, you know everything about me. I was born in New Canaan, Connecticut. I was an only child when my parents were killed. My biggest challenge growing up?"

August expected she would say losing her parents so young and growing up an orphan.

Kathleen tapped her lips. "A hard one. I've always been able to manage challenges for a positive result."

August leaned forward. "Surely the loss of your parents caused you struggles growing up."

"Of course that, but one has to go on, right? Before my mother was killed, my biggest challenge was competing for her attention. She had a very magnetic personality. Everyone who knew her was in love with her. I craved her undivided attention, but I always felt frustrated. She seemed just out of reach. She should have belonged exclusively to me, her only child." Kathleen absentmindedly touched the scar at her hairline.

"Number Four, what would I change? I would make the agoraphobia go away. It's infuriating that I can't control it." She took August's hands in hers. "Do you know I haven't had a panic attack since we met?" She brought August's hand to her lips and kissed her knuckle. "Now it's your turn to answer."

August squirmed and cleared her throat. "I more often ask questions than answer them, but here goes. I was born in Lake Placid. My parents were vacationing there, and I came along ahead of schedule. As soon as my mother and I could travel, we came home to the city. I've lived here all my life, even during college and law school. The next question...?"

"Siblings."

"Oh, right. I was an only child. My mother was forty-one years old when I was born. My parents were completely surprised when they found out she was pregnant. The best medical minds in the city told them they wouldn't be able to have children. I have lots of cousins on my mother's side, mostly in Boston, but I never experienced the give and take and struggle for attention and identity I suppose one has growing up with brothers and sisters."

"Number three. Your biggest challenge growing up."

August shook her head. "I have to dig deep for that one. I suppose my greatest challenge growing up is related to being an only child. I'm a fourth-generation lawyer on my father's side. My grandfather and father expected I would go to law school. As far back as I can remember, they drilled into my consciousness that I'd been blessed with a good brain and material abundance, and it was my responsibility to make the world a better place through practicing law."

"Why would you see living up to that expectation as a great challenge? You're doing what they expected. I'm an example of your compassion. Look how you're helping me."

"I've translated their expectations into a compulsion to rush to the rescue, to untie the damsel from the railroad tracks just in the nick of time. In my head, I think of it as my Wonder Woman complex."

"Surely rescuing people is not a problem. It's commendable."

"Not everyone wants to be rescued. Anyway, let's not turn this into a therapy session. Next question."

"One thing you'd like to change about yourself."

August glanced at Kathleen. "Being an attorney means approaching the world from an analytical point of view, suppressing emotions. That's certainly my nature. How much of my temperament is nature and how much nurture, I can't say. I tend to analyze everything, and I'm almost never spontaneous. Sometimes I think I'm not a very passionate person. Other people seem to feel things more deeply than I do. Things like causes and beliefs."

"And relationships?"

"Yes. Maybe I'm missing out on an important part of the human experience."

"Haven't you ever been madly in love?"

"I was once, but I was young and too focused on my career and trying to live the script my grandfather and father had written for me. I regret that I let the relationship slip through my fingers."

Kathleen laughed. "I've been madly in love dozens of times."

"'In love' is a very imprecise term."

"I see what you mean about analyzing everything. So you'd like to change that part of your temperament? To be more spontaneous?"

August wondered if this beautiful woman could inspire her passion.

Kathleen leaned in and took August's face in her hands, pressing her into the couch with her body. "For now, just feel, don't think." She kissed her hard on the mouth. Her lipstick was fruit flavored, peaches or plums, and her breath was hot and clean tasting with a hint of the wine.

August tried to sit up. Kathleen pushed her back and straddled her lap. "I want to see you underneath this." She pulled the tail of her blouse from her slacks, opened the top two buttons, and stripped the blouse over her head. She unhooked her bra, leaned back against August's thighs, and sighed. "Beautiful. I thought so."

"You've been speculating about my breasts?"

Kathleen nodded and took a breast in each of her palms. "How they'd look and how they'd feel." She bent over and blew against her nipples, sending a wave of nerve current through August's body. "And how they would taste." She took a nipple between her lips.

"Kathleen, wait."

She put a finger across August's lips. "Too much talking." Kathleen led her across the room to the bed and pushed her onto her back. She stripped off her own dress and underclothes, and straddled August.

The wind dashed rain against the windowpane next to the bed. August wondered if water was blowing in the open window by the kitchen, and if the game hens in the oven would burn. She forced her mind to focus on the firm buttock beneath her left palm and the silky feel of Kathleen's skin under the probing fingers of her right hand. Kathleen's pearls reflected lights from across the street as they bounced against her chest in rhythm with her thrusts. Kathleen bent over for a deep kiss, and the pearls brushed across August's face. They were warm from being next to Kathleen's skin and seemed almost alive. Kathleen pressed hard against August's hand and cried out as she climaxed.

The grandfather clock struck the half hour. Kathleen whispered in her ear. "Turn over." She pulled down August's jeans and panties. Somewhere, in spite of agoraphobia, Kathleen had become an expert in pleasuring a woman with her hands and mouth. She knew exactly where to stroke and caress for maximum effect. Maybe she learned from some of the dozens of times she'd been "madly in love."

She brought August to the edge of orgasm then backed off, teasing, "Not yet." August moaned and pressed Kathleen's hand into her and heard the roar in her ears and felt the dam burst of sensations signaling her orgasm. She fell against the pillow. She groaned. "Water."

Kathleen threw on a robe and padded barefoot to the kitchen and came back with a tumbler of ice water. She went to an armoire and brought a burgundy silk robe for August. She sat cross-legged on the bed and watched her drain the glass of water. She stroked the smooth fabric covering August's nipple. "Another?" She chuckled. "Glass of water, I mean."

August looked at her over the rim of the tumbler. Kathleen was suppressing a smirk. "What's that look about? What are you thinking?"

"I'm thinking of your rule about keeping things professional between us. This is what I've wanted, to be more than a client to you."

Jane Alden

Chapter Eight

AUGUST DROPPED HER PENCIL and rested her chin in her hand. She relived the events of the night before with Kathleen. She thought of the points in the evening where she could have put a stop to things. In the first place, she should have declined the dinner invitation. Being honest with herself, she knew ahead of time she'd be walking into temptation. Then that game, Four Questions. She didn't have to play along. She shouldn't have disclosed personal information to Kathleen. And she certainly could have drawn the line after the first kiss.

Lena stuck her head in the door. "It's June on the line."

Lena always had an edge to her voice when August's ex was involved. She once told August that June couldn't be as smart as everyone thought since she let August get away. No matter how many times August told her the breakup was mutual, Lena still clucked her tongue and said, "Whatever."

August stretched. "Put her through."

Lena pursed her lips and pulled the door closed.

"Hello, June. If you're asking, I'm still trying to decide which lesbian bucket I fall into, basketball or eighteenth-century music."

June chuckled. "I'm calling last minute. Can you meet for lunch?"

August looked at her watch. "If we go now and keep it short. I'm backed up with work."

"How about the Washington Square Hotel. Just down the street from you. See you in twenty minutes?"

August ran a comb through her hair, applied fresh lipstick, and walked the three blocks from her office to the hotel. In the restaurant, the maître d' showed her to a two-person table by the large front window. He held August's chair, snapped her napkin open with a flourish, and draped it across her lap. "May I bring you something from the bar, madam?"

"A club soda with lime."

After a few minutes, June bustled in, dropped into the chair across from August, and eyed the club soda. "I need something stiffer." She ordered a martini and took a healthy sip when the drink arrived. "That's good. What a week. All my clients are scrambling to beat the end of the year tax reckoning. It's the same every year this time."

August nodded. "I'm crazy busy too. I think men try and divorce their wives this time of the year for financial reasons too. Somehow their cheating always gets found out around Thanksgiving." She waited, sensing June was itching to bring up a subject having nothing to do with their law practices.

June stirred her drink with the olive. "I have a motive for inviting you to lunch. It's my treat, by the way. I need a willing ear to complain to."

"Go ahead. Willing and able."

June glanced up. "It's about a woman."

"Why am I not surprised?"

June grabbed August's arm. "This is serious. She's sending me all kinds of signals, notes and phone calls, but when I try to get closer, she backs off. It's come hither, go away. She's driving me mad."

August resisted the urge to smile. "You're used to a quick surrender. Maybe she's playing you. Remember the time we went deep-sea fishing? What you describe reminds me of the struggle between you and that tuna you hooked. Except he got away."

"Don't make fun of me. I'm in real distress here."

"You're right. I'm sorry." August held up a finger. "The waiter's coming. Hold the thought." She looked over her menu. "Don't forget, I have to make this fast. You can't order your usual soufflé or something else complicated and time-consuming."

"You order for both of us so you can't complain."

August closed the menu. "Two Denver omelets, not too well done, and two glasses of Chardonnay." She watched the waiter hurry toward the kitchen. "And when we've solved your woman problem, I have one of my own to discuss."

June drained her martini. "Well, that sounds juicy, but can we take mine first?"

"Carry on."

"She'll hardly let me see her and when she does, only in her apartment. She won't go out with me. I'm beginning to think she's embarrassed to be seen with me in public."

August felt a foreboding heaviness in the pit of her stomach.

"Why are you holding your mouth in that funny way you do when you're upset? Am I annoying you with my complaining?"

"Who is this woman?"

"You know her. Kathleen O'Brien, the case I referred to you."

August's mouth fell open. "That's impossible. She's been chasing me around her apartment for days, and, I'm embarrassed to admit, I let myself get caught."

"By that I'm assuming you mean you went to bed with her."

August felt her cheeks flush. She nodded. "Yes, just last night. I've been beating myself up all morning about it. How did this come about?"

"She sent me a card with her phone number, just after you and I talked when you were in Lake Placid. She thanked me for recommending you and praised you to high heaven. Called you her savior. I felt curious to see how she'd grown up. I told you I used to babysit her. Three weeks ago I called her, and she invited me to her apartment for dinner. Things took off from there."

"She's never said a word about seeing you."

"Does she know about our history, yours and mine?"

August shook her head. "Not from me."

The waiter interrupted with their food and wine. June stopped him. "Bring me another martini." She picked up her fork and pushed the omelet around the plate. "Does she go out in public with you?"

"She has agoraphobia, a fear of having a panic attack in most public places. She hasn't told you about her problem?"

June shook her head. "No, but it explains a lot." She took a healthy sip of her martini. "Knowing this is a relief in a way. Now I've got a good reason to steer clear of Miss O'Brien."

August gazed out the window. "Don't decide that on my account. I should never have let it happen. I feel embarrassed and angry with myself."

June took August's hand across the table. "Whatever. Your friendship is more important to me than any woman. You have to admit, though, she is hot!"

Chapter Nine

THE NEXT MORNING, AUGUST sat across the desk from Louis Collins in his office on the second floor of the Whitney Museum of Modern Art. He fingered the business card. "August Mapes, Attorney at Law. This is a very lovely card. It sends exactly the right message of competence and taste."

"Thank you." She looked around the office. "I could say exactly the same about this room." The natural wood desk, chairs, and sleek conference table had clean lines. Spotlights illuminated paintings spaced around the eggshell-white walls. The paintings and an expensive-looking antique oriental carpet provided the only color and pattern in the room.

"I like to treat the office as a miniature exhibition space. I rotate the works every month or so. This artist is Millard Sheets, a California watercolorist, from his dark period in India during the war. Are you interested in art? I'd love to give you a tour of the museum, but don't let me digress. You're here on business. My niece alerted me to expect your call. She's absolutely dazzled by you."

August flashed back to the sensation of Kathleen's lips on her breast. She squirmed in her seat. "I want to help her. I'm here because you might help too."

"For my beloved niece, I'll do anything I can. She didn't give me any details about the matter. She said it's a case of a difficult editing client."

She took a legal pad and pencil from her briefcase. "We're trying to track down an author with unclear motives. He's corresponding with Kathleen under an alias. He appears to know quite a lot about her life, including the accident that killed her parents and possibly her time at school. He has some connection with incidents in her past. May I ask a few questions about the time after Kathleen's parents' death?"

Louis nodded. "It was a terrible time for all of us."

"I know her father was a successful real estate developer. The family was well-liked and active in New Canaan. Tell me about her mother, your sister."

Louis's hand shook as he lit a cigarette with a slim gold lighter. "It's difficult for me, even after all these years. I adored Francine. Everyone adored her. She lit up a room with her outgoing personality, but not in a self-centered way. She had a talent for putting people at ease."

"She sounds remarkable."

"She was. My sister excelled at everything she put her hand to." He ticked off Francine's accomplishment on his fingers. "She threw legendary parties. She won the golf championship at their country club. She played piano beautifully. Francine and William married before she finished Barnard. She made a lovely home for him. After Kathleen came, she turned all her attention to becoming the world's best mother."

Louis stubbed out his cigarette in a crystal ashtray. "When I got the call about their accident, my mind just rejected it. She was so strong. This sounds crazy, but my first thought was, 'Not Francine. She just wouldn't let that happen.' As though she could have pulled out her magic lasso like Wonder Woman and stopped the collision." He took a monogrammed handkerchief from his pocket and dabbed his eyes and cleared his throat. "Sorry."

"I know this is painful. You're aware the driver of the car, David Gates, died recently."

"Kathleen told me. A suicide."

"That's the official word."

"You have some question about it?" He folded his handkerchief carefully and put it back in his pocket. "Never mind answering that. How he died doesn't matter to me."

"I understand your feelings. The accident was a terrible tragedy for your family, not only your niece but also you and your sister Carole." She consulted her notes. "I'd like to ask you about after the accident, when you and Carole became guardians for Kathleen."

70

"I was twenty years old, still in college. Carole and Francine are quite a bit older than I. Carole was sixteen and Francine fifteen when I was born." He turned and picked up a framed photo from the credenza behind him, a studio shot of two teenaged girls, one standing with her hand on the shoulder of the other. The seated girl held a toddler in her lap.

He handed August the photo. "That's Carole standing behind Francine and me. I was about a year and a half in that picture."

Carole was gorgeous, with perfect features, dark hair, and light eyes. Her remote expression in the photo implied she would have preferred to be someplace else. The other young woman, Francine, was beautiful too, but her looks seemed more accessible—and somehow more interesting—than her sister's, like a slightly imperfect copy. She was blond. Her grey eyes were a little too close together for perfection. Her smile was open and radiant, showing a slight overbite. The little boy, in knickers and a bow tie, gazed adoringly up at her instead of at the camera.

August handed the photo back. "A beautiful family."

He set the photo in place on the credenza carefully. His hand lingered on the frame for a moment. "Carole has beauty and brains. She was a champion equestrian as a teenager. In spite of her gifts and being the older sister, she was always jealous of Francine, of her way with people. Carole was Valedictorian, Francine was Most Popular.

"Carole was in her mid-thirties when Francine died. Single then and still is, and very much a career woman. She owns a successful interior design firm which was just getting started back then. She had no intention of raising a nine-year-old child. She took charge of finding Kathleen a boarding school in Manhattan. I went along with her decision, but after one term, I moved Kathleen to a different school, over Carole's strong objections. After that, she washed her hands of us."

"Kathleen used those exact words."

"I may have put the phrase in her head, but it's true."

"So you are still estranged from your sister."

"Yes. The more time goes by, the more ridiculous the situation seems. There are only the three of us left, Carole, Kathleen, and myself. We should be supporting each other. The whole disagreement about Kathleen's school was twenty years ago."

August sat forward in her chair. "Tell me about your decision to move Kathleen to a different school, Mr. Collins."

He searched her face. "I'm going to trust your discretion, Miss Mapes, in order to help my niece. Kathleen told me a priest at the school was taking special notice of her, giving her treats, reading to her at night, consoling her about her parents' death. She said his behavior was making her uncomfortable. I felt concerned his attention was inappropriate, that he might be sexually abusing her, or leading up to it anyway. I went to Carole with my suspicions and told her we should take Kathleen out of the school. Carole questioned Kathleen about the priest. Afterward, Carole insisted he was just being kind and refused to consider a different school."

"And you disagreed."

He lit another cigarette. "I had seen the signs before." He looked August in the eye through the smoke from his cigarette. She watched him weigh whether to go on. "I recognized the signs because the same thing happened to me. I was determined not to allow my niece's abuse."

"I'm sorry. I know how difficult admitting that must be."

He shrugged. "I've come to grips with it after much therapy, but that's a longer story for another time. I refused to let go of the matter about the priest at Kathleen's school. I told Carole I'd report my suspicions to the headmistress, even though I had no real proof. I went to her office. She was a senile old bat who barely knew her own name. She was clearly not going to do anything. Then I threatened to go to the police. The prospect jolted Carole. She stood aside while I found another school."

"So you, Carole, the headmistress. Can you think of anyone else who might have known about your suspicions?"

He shook his head.

"You didn't go to the police."

"I regret the decision now. Kathleen cried and begged me not to. The knowledge the priest may be abusing some other little girl as we speak haunts me. I've heard the school shut down a few years ago, but who knows where he could have moved?"

"Do you remember his name?"

"I'll never forget it. Father Anthony Laurette."

Chapter Ten

AFTER HER MEETING WITH Louis Collins, August hurried back to her office. A stack of pink telephone messages waited in the middle of her desk. She blew a stray lock of hair out of her eyes and began sorting the message slips by priority. Her first call was to Blackie. She put him on the trail of the priest from Our Lady of the Assumption. "E. Gamin delivered another chapter about the murder of a priest. I need you to track down Father Anthony Laurette. He was at Our Lady of the Assumption school twenty years ago. His life may be in jeopardy."

Lena stuck her head in the door. "Miss O'Brien on the phone. She says it's urgent."

August picked up the phone. "Kathleen, I can't talk right now. I'm terribly behind."

"I'm sorry." She heard the same edge of panic underneath Kathleen's voice as the first time they talked on the phone. "He's delivered another envelope to my door. I don't understand, and I'm frightened. If you can't come to my apartment, will you meet me halfway in the park? I promise to be quick."

"All right." August hung up and tossed a wave over her shoulder as she hurried past Lena. "Back in a minute."

She ran into the park around a crowd listening to a jazz combo playing for tips. Kathleen was already waiting on a bench beside the main walkway bisecting the park. She stood up when she spotted August hurrying down the path. "Thank goodness you could come. Look at this."

Kathleen shook a card the size of a playing card from a plain white envelope. One side of the card showed a photograph of an elderly man in a priest's collar, and underneath the picture: "Padre Anthony Laurette, Nacido 31 de agosto 1887, Murio 20 de octubre 1952, Iglesia San Juan." On the back of the card: "La Oración del Señor." The Lord's Prayer in Spanish.

Kathleen sat down on the bench. "It's a funeral card written in Spanish. Now that I see his picture, I recognize him as the priest from Our Lady of the Assumption. I think the funeral card says he died the twentieth of October, two weeks ago, at the Church of San Juan, but it doesn't say where the church is. What does it mean?"

"I'm not sure. There's no address on the envelope. Any note this time?"

Kathleen shook her head.

"You're sure E. Gamin left the card?"

"Yes. Well, I assume it was he. I don't know for sure who left it."

August put the card back in the envelope and slipped it in her blazer pocket. She pulled the blazer closer around her body, wishing she had worn a heavier coat. "I met with your Uncle Louis today."

"He's wonderful, isn't he?"

"He cares for you very much, and wants to help. He was incredibly forthcoming. One detail I didn't understand. He said you were uncomfortable with Father Anthony's attention. That surprised me. You told me that at the time you thought the priest was just being kind. Your uncle said you knew he was considering going to the police about his suspicions the priest was abusing you, and you begged him not to involve them. He didn't report Laurette, something he bitterly regrets to this day. You gave me the impression you didn't discuss being uncomfortable with the priest's attentions with your uncle."

"I must have been confused."

"Understandable, I suppose. Do you remember your aunt Carole questioning you about Father Anthony before your uncle took you out of Our Lady of the Assumption?"

"No. She may have. I'm not sure."

Two nannies pushed black prams along the path past them.

"I edited the chapter and mailed it back, as you said. This card proves the chapter anticipates the murder of Father Anthony, doesn't it? I don't understand why it was written in Spanish."

August took the card from her pocket and looked at both sides again. "I don't know. My investigator is working on finding Father Anthony. He'll come up with some answers."

Kathleen put her hand on August's arm and left it there. "You've coaxed me from my apartment. That's a good sign, isn't it?" She edged closer so their thighs touched. "I've been thinking about the other night." Kathleen chuckled. "I guess we proved you don't lack passion after all."

August's body tensed. She scooted away from Kathleen's touch. "Why haven't you mentioned seeing June Fleming?"

"I suppose it just never came up. Should I have?"

"I was surprised when she told me."

"I'm so grateful to her for the referral to you. I invited her over for dinner, and I've seen her a few times since." Kathleen searched her face. "You're more than just colleagues, aren't you?"

"We met in law school, and we were in a relationship for a while."

"You lived together? She didn't tell me that." She patted August's arm and left her hand there. "Let's not talk about June." She stroked the rough wool of August's sleeve. "If you can spare a little more time, we could go for a drink somewhere. Have you been to L's? It's nice, a pleasant crowd. It's just around the corner on Bleeker."

"I know the place, but aren't you afraid of having an attack?"

"If you're with me, I think I'll feel in control. It will be good practice being in public, for when I have to meet with the police. We can make sure to get a table close to the door." Kathleen stood and smoothed her skirt. "So, L's?"

August thought about the pink telephone messages on her desk back in the office and her promise to Lena she'd be right back. "I simply can't spare the time now." She held up her thumb and index finger. "There's a stack of phone messages this thick in the middle of my desk. Plus, I'm interviewing your aunt later this afternoon."

"Why are you meeting with Aunt Carole? I've told you she and I are not in contact."

"E. Gamin appears to have a connection to events in your childhood. Your aunt may be able to shed some light on that."

Kathleen nodded. "That makes sense. Just take what she says with a grain of salt. She's not my biggest fan." She put her hand on August's arm again. "Can I have a rain check for L's?"

"We'll see."

August rushed back across the park and up the front stoop to her office. Lena looked up from her typewriter. "New phone messages are in a separate stack. I indicated the ones that are second calls."

August added the new messages to the old and dived in. By two o'clock, only one was left, from Blackie Rye. The message said he had developments on the priest's death to report.

"Lena, please see if Blackie can come right over."

***

Blackie settled into the chair across from August.

She grabbed her pad and pencil. "You have results already?"

"It's all about who you know. I've got a connection with the Archdiocese through my cousin, and wait till you hear where my discussion with him led. The Archdiocese transferred Father Anthony Laurette when Our Lady of the Assumption school closed three years ago. They reassigned him to a small church in Chiapas, in southern Mexico, about as far away from Manhattan as you can get. My cousin couldn't find out whether Father Anthony requested the remote assignment or whether they were trying to get him out of sight.

"Then I called my contact in Mexico. He's a retiree like me from NYPD who does some detective work part time for American corporations in Mexico and Central America. He tries every so often to convince me to move down there. Says it's paradise and good money, but the situation sounds a little on the dicey side for my taste. Anyway, that area of Mexico is known for internecine fighting over protection of the rainforest."

August looked up from her notes and smiled at Blackie.

"What?"

"Do you know how few people in the world know the definition of the word 'internecine,' let alone how to use it in a sentence? No wonder they call you The Professor."

"Just don't ask me to spell it. Anyway, they're fighting among themselves. One group wants to bulldoze the whole thing for agricultural purposes and the other, an outfit called the Liberation Army of the South, wants to keep the forest pristine. Officially, the Church tries to stay neutral, but apparently Father Anthony was pretty outspoken in favor of the local farmers.

"Two weeks ago, the nuns called the Federales to the village of Aldama, population twelve hundred seventy-three souls, where they found Father Anthony hanging in his bedroom in the rectory."

August shuddered. "That explains this." She handed the funeral card across the desk. "Someone, probably E. Gamin, left it at Miss O'Brien's door."

Blackie turned the card over in his hand and nodded. "The Federales think the hanging was the work of the Liberation Army. Either the Archdiocese doesn't know about the incident yet, or they're keeping his death under wraps."

"Could the murder be the work of E. Gamin?"

"I suppose he could have paid someone to do the deed. Hiring a paid assassin would be fairly easy in that part of the world. Not likely he would have gone all that way to murder the priest personally, then come back this soon to hand-deliver the funeral card to Miss O'Brien."

August paced between her desk and the window. "Do you think the case of Father Laurette clears our football player as a suspect in the death of David Gates? There doesn't appear to be any connection between Tobias and the priest."

"He may have kept track of Miss O'Brien after the accident, though he denied that when we met with him. Or we may have more than one killer on our hands."

"Do you mean a conspiracy?"

"I don't know what I mean." Blackie paused. "I do know we badly need to get NYPD involved."

"I agree." She checked her watch. "I have an appointment in half an hour with Miss O'Brien's aunt. I'll call you afterward, and we can plan how to approach NYPD." She showed Blackie out and gathered up her notes and the file. The funeral card fell out on her desk. She stared at the photograph of the elderly priest. Was he a child molester, or a victim in the drama that was Kathleen O'Brien's life?

Chapter Eleven

COLLINS DESIGN OCCUPIED AN entire floor in a midtown high-rise, across from Bryant Park on the edge of the garment district. The security guard at a desk in the lobby checked August's driver's license against the approved visitor list. She wondered what state secrets an interior design firm might be protecting. The guard nodded toward a grouping of leather chairs, indicating she should join several men waiting for appointments in the offices upstairs.

Before she could sit, a young woman with a bouncy ponytail dressed in a straight black skirt and turtleneck appeared. "Miss Mapes?"

"Yes."

She offered her hand. "I'm Monica, Miss Collins's executive assistant. This way, please."

August thought about Lena, who refused to answer to anything other than "secretary." She pictured her at her typewriter, working away in their informal little office in the Village. August made a mental note to describe Monica's air of officious self-importance to Lena. She'd find it funny.

They rode the elevator in silence. Monica showed her into Carole Collins's office. The room could have been a carbon copy of her brother Louis's at the Whitney Museum. White walls, blond furniture with stark lines, oriental carpets on the floor. Instead of artworks, building schematics lined the walls. A huge conference table in the middle of the room overflowed with fabric swatches, paint color cards, and open wallpaper sample books. On a credenza behind the desk, there was a photograph of a young rider astride her horse, clearing a jump in a steeplechase course.

Carole Collins stood up to greet her. She was tall and thin, and her black business suit was perfectly tailored and understated. August had expected a mature version of the beautiful teenager in Louis's photograph. With time, Carole's features had settled into sharp, chiseled angles. Her dark hair was shot through with grey, and her eyes were crystal blue. Her looks were still arresting and in a way more interesting than when she was a teenager.

She held up a finger. "Excuse me one second, Miss Mapes." She called Monica over and gave her a few quick instructions.

August took the opportunity to study some of the plans on the wall. They appeared to be representations of large, commercial buildings.

Carole handed Monica a stack of papers. "And Monica, hold the interruptions while Miss Mapes and I talk." Carole walked over and stood behind August. The faint scent of Chanel No. 5 teased August's nose.

"You're looking at the new San Francisco ballet hall. It's consuming all my time right now. The design committee of the board, wealthy women with too much time on their hands and homosexual men, fancy themselves better designers than I."

"I assumed you design private homes."

"Oh, no. Commercial design is far more lucrative, and satisfying the client is much easier. The decision makers generally have more interest in deadlines and budgets than in second-guessing my designs. I gave up residential projects some time ago."

"I suspect you give up some visibility, though."

"You mean my name doesn't show up in the society pages. Fine with me. I'm not much of a public person. Please sit." She gestured toward two chairs flanking an amoeba-shaped coffee table topped with glass.

"I've talked with your brother. He mentioned your accomplishments as a horsewoman. I noticed the photograph behind your desk."

Carole turned to look at the picture. "Yes, that was some years ago."

"Do you still ride?"

"I don't compete anymore, but I ride three times a week in Central Park. It keeps me grounded."

"I'll admit I've always been a little afraid of horses. And the jumping must carry some danger with it."

"It can. Of course, you train for it. Can we get you anything? Coffee, tea?" Carole Collins wasn't interested in small talk. August could sense she wanted to dispense with this discussion as quickly as she could.

"No, thanks. I appreciate your time. You mentioned difficult clients, and I'm representing your niece with her own difficult client."

"I hope you haven't wasted your time. My niece and I aren't in touch. Apart from some business matters my attorney handles, left over from her parents' death, Kathleen and I don't communicate."

"So I understand." August sat on the edge of her seat. She needed to establish some kind of rapport with this icy woman. "Kathleen could be in danger. An individual who may have murdered two people is stalking her. He appears to hold the misguided idea he's seeking retribution for offenses against her."

"If she's in danger, I assume she's gone to the police."

"We haven't yet. Do you know about Kathleen's agoraphobia?"

"As I said, my niece and I don't communicate. I know Kathleen is a deeply disturbed person. Has been since she was a child. So agoraphobia doesn't surprise me."

August remembered Kathleen's remark about taking her aunt's comments with a grain of salt. She let the remark lie. "The murders have been made to appear as suicide or the result of civil unrest. And they didn't happen in New York, so we want to have as strong a set of facts as possible before we involve the NYPD."

"What makes you suspect the deaths aren't as they appear?"

"This author stalking Kathleen is writing stories in the first person from the point of view of the killer. He changes the names and other details, but the facts closely mirror those of actual deaths."

Carole stood and walked to her desk. "Excuse me just a moment." She picked up the phone. "Monica, we're going to be longer than I expected. Reschedule my appointment with the architect on the Pierre Hotel project. And please bring us some tea."

She took her seat again. "Go on."

August took out her notes. "First, I need to fill in more detail. An anonymous individual retained Kathleen to edit a book. He has sent her two chapters so far. In each, the author recounts a murder in eerie detail and in first person. Chapter One is about the staged suicide of a victim very much resembling the man who caused the accident that killed your sister and brother-in-law. The New Canaan police found David Gates dead of carbon monoxide poisoning in his garage. A few days later, Kathleen received a chapter in the mail describing the murder, in the killer's own words."

"I hope you haven't come to my place of business expecting me to work up any sympathy for him. As far as I'm concerned, it's just desserts and twenty years too late coming. He caused a terrible accident then fled the scene while my sister bled to death."

August shifted in her seat. She suspected this severe woman was used to dominating people and situations. She'd be damned if she'd let Carole intimidate her. "Understandable. I'm not after sympathy for Mr. Gates. I'm here to represent my client, your niece, in a matter that might present some danger for her. I hope you can shed some light on it."

Monica interrupted with a tray of tea and cookies. Carole poured two cups and passed one to August. "If it were later in the day, I'd suggest something stronger."

"And I'd take you up on it."

Carole poured cream in her tea and stirred it. "I apologize for my harsh reaction. I know you're only doing your job."

August was encouraged that she could back the woman down. She nodded. "The second chapter was hand-delivered to Kathleen's apartment. The story describes the murder of a priest at a Catholic girls' school. A day or so after the chapter appeared at Kathleen's door, someone, we assume the writer, delivered this." She handed Carole the funeral card.

Carole looked at both sides. "Father Anthony. Twenty years ago, he was at Our Lady of the Assumption school."

August nodded. "We tracked down the priest. The Mexican police discovered Father Anthony Laurette two weeks ago, hanging in the rectory of his church in southern Mexico. Kathleen's anonymous author changed the setting and the facts in his story, but the outcome was the same."

Carole passed the funeral card back. "Since you've spoken with Louis, I assume you want my side of the Father Anthony story." She checked her watch. "It's late enough for that drink. For this discussion, I really do need it." She rose and walked to a sideboard in the corner of the office. She pulled the stopper from a crystal decanter, poured two drinks, and placed one in front of August.

"My sister and I were very close in age—I'm older by less than a year—but we were very different in temperament. The differences contributed to some epic clashes, but I still loved her fiercely. When Louis came along, surprising us all, Francine and I were teenagers. My sister practically adopted him as her own baby. They remained close until her death. Louis may feel he owns more of the pain and grief than I do." She looked in August's eyes, as though hoping for some details about August's talk with Louis. Carole turned away and dabbed at her eyes. "Sorry. Give me a moment. You would think after twenty years..."

August sipped her drink. "The loss of Francine was a tragedy for both you and Louis."

Carol cleared her throat. "When my sister and her husband died, responsibility for Kathleen passed to me and Louis. He was only twenty, in college, and clueless about what to do with a nine-year-old girl. He deferred to me. I found her a place in a fine school near me in the city, Our Lady of the Assumption. Father Anthony was the priest there. Kathleen didn't do well from the beginning. She bridled against the rules and regimentation and had trouble making friends among the other girls. She begged me to move her to another school. The headmistress recommended we give Kathleen some time to adjust. After all, she had just lost her parents.

"Before the end of the term, Louis called me absolutely distraught. Kathleen had told him Father Anthony was abusing her. He insisted we go to the headmistress, even the police, with her accusations. I was traveling between New York and the west coast, but I dropped everything to get to the bottom of it."

It was clear to August that Carole Collins was anxious August believe she had acted responsibly.

"Kathleen repeated her accusations when I questioned her. She didn't use the words 'sexual abuse,' of course, but she described Father Anthony paying special attention to her, consoling her about her parents' death, praying with her, but she denied Father Anthony had touched her.

"Louis and I met with the headmistress. She was very disturbed by the prospect the priest might be acting inappropriately. She called him into her office on the spot. The confrontation was uncomfortable, accusing the priest of such an act. He denied anything inappropriate. Said he noticed Kathleen struggling to fit in at the school. His heart went out to her. He seemed horrified he had made Kathleen feel uncomfortable. He offered his resignation."

"Did the headmistress accept?"

"I couldn't say how the headmistress dealt with him in the end. Louis was dissatisfied with the meeting and intended to go to the police. I think Kathleen became frightened and begged him not to. Louis dropped the police idea but was determined to find a different school, which he did. He lashed out at me, accusing me of taking the school's side against the family. My relationship with my brother and my niece ended there."

"You don't believe Father Anthony was abusing Kathleen."

"No, I'm certain he was not. I believe Kathleen manipulated Louis to get her way, to get him to move her to a different school."

There was a soft knock on the door, and Monica stuck her head in. "Your next appointment is here, Miss Collins."

August placed her notes in her briefcase. "Thank you for seeing me."

"I'm afraid we're ending this as we began. I hope you haven't wasted your time."

August started toward the door and paused. "I have one last question, Miss Collins. Why did you agree to see me?"

"I wish only the best for Kathleen. You seem to be sincerely trying to help my niece. I'll just say one more thing that may make the trip uptown worth your time. Be very careful of being manipulated."

Jane Alden

Chapter Twelve

L'S WAS ON THE first floor of a narrow red brick townhouse from the 1800s, sandwiched between two pre-war apartment buildings.

August and June had sometimes gone to the bar with friends when they were in law school. L's had a reputation for being safer than most bars catering to lesbians. It was rumored to be owned by the Mafia, and the word was they paid off whoever necessary in order to avoid raids, not out of any urge to protect their clients, but because the threat of police storming the front door was bad for business.

Kathleen led the way through the double front doors into a dimly lit interior. The lone spot of light came from a jukebox against one wall, outlined with rainbow neon, beyond a postage stamp dance floor. The dance floor was empty, except for one couple swaying to Billie Holiday's "Moonglow."

Well-dressed women occupied the barstools and about half the tables ringing the dance floor. Their heads turned in unison toward Kathleen and August. Several gave Kathleen a wave and a smile and August an appraising glance.

Kathleen steered them toward an empty table in the corner by the front door and scooted their chairs as close together as possible.

August looked around the room. The bar hadn't changed much since her law school days. If anything, the patrons looked younger and the ambiance felt more relaxed. She guessed her impressions of changes in the bar were a sign of her age and of the more open atmosphere for women following the war. "You come here often."

"I used to, before the panic attacks." She held up a finger. "I'll be right back." She crossed the corner of the dance floor to the bar and returned with a martini in each hand. She dropped into her chair. "Now this is nice. Thank you for agreeing to come with me. No talk about E. Gamin, okay?" She raised her glass. "To passion." She clicked the rim of August's glass.

August took a tentative sip and cleared her throat. She was unaccustomed to the strong liquor.

"Tell me about Lake Placid. You seem to really love the place. I noticed a difference in you between the first time we met before your trip and when you came back to town. You were much calmer."

"It's the one place in the world I can really relax." August described the picturesque main street overlooking the lake, both practically deserted in the early fall. As August talked, Kathleen began almost absentmindedly stroking her thigh under the table in time to the mellow blues from the jukebox.

August squirmed under her touch. "This time of the year is ideal. The weather is perfect, brisk but not frigid. I spent some time canoeing, which was just heavenly. You can paddle all day and never see another soul. Sometimes you're lucky enough to catch a glimpse of a moose getting a drink from the lake."

"Did you ski while you were there?"

"It was too early for snow. I did ride the ski lift up Whiteface Mountain and hike down. They run the lift all summer and fall for hikers."

"And all this was by yourself? I'd love to see it. Maybe we can go there together sometime." She glanced at August's glass. "Drink up so we can have another. I picture you bolting out the door if I can't keep you captured."

They drained their glasses, and Kathleen went to the bar for more martinis. August watched her exchange a few words with an attractive woman sitting on a stool at the end of the bar. The woman put her hand on Kathleen's arm. Kathleen picked up the drinks and turned away, starting back to the table. She jerked her arm out of the woman's grasp, almost spilling the drinks.

August nodded toward the bar. "Who is she?"

"Oh, just someone I used to see here, when I came before."

The front door opened, letting a rectangle of pale sunlight cut through the blue haze of cigarette smoke. A group of four women, laughing and talking loudly, paused a moment for their eyes to adjust, then found stools at the bar. As August and Kathleen sipped their drinks, other women drifted through the front door in singles and couples. Soon, all the seats in the bar were taken, and several women were standing. The music changed from soothing to upbeat and loud.

August drained the last of her martini. "Well..."

Kathleen had to lean in to be heard. "Not yet. Tell me about your Lake Placid house."

August described the rambling, brown-shingled cabin with its warm and comfortable great room and second-floor porch overlooking the pines and the lake. Her tongue felt thick from the gin.

Kathleen's hand moved to stroking her inner thigh. She whispered in August's ear. "Do you ever have fantasies?"

August chewed her olive. "I do. Is this about to be another game like Four Questions?"

Kathleen smiled. "I've been having a fantasy about you. We're sitting in a crowded place, like now, and I'm doing things to you without anyone knowing."

August looked around the crowded bar. She felt several women were watching the two of them closely. Or maybe it was the gin making her feel paranoid. She should never drink gin.

Kathleen chuckled. "Your nipples are hard." She unzipped the fly of August's slacks under the table. She whispered in August's ear. "In my fantasy, you want to moan but you can't because someone might hear. You want me to stop, but at the same time you hope I won't." She slid her hand inside August's pants and began fondling her.

The crowd noises and music blurred in August's ears. "Stop, Kathleen. Not here."

Kathleen encircled her hips with one arm and with the other hand began stroking her throbbing, most sensitive nerve endings with her thumbnail.

"I said..." She gripped Kathleen's wrist and moved her hand away. "Stop."

Kathleen's mouth turned up in the half smirk that August recognized. "But you said you want to be more spontaneous."

August gritted her teeth and felt an embarrassed flush creep across her cheeks. She zipped her pants. "Not like that. Let's go." She scraped her chair back and headed unsteadily through the crowd toward the door.

They walked toward Kathleen's apartment building without speaking. The cold air cleared August's head a little. She walked faster.

Kathleen caught hold of her arm. "Slow down."

August pulled her arm away. "No."

"You're upset. I don't understand. It was just a fantasy. I thought you'd—"

August interrupted her. "Your fantasy, not mine. You were treating me like an object. You were trying to control me. Some women may get turned on by it, but I'm not one of them. You put me in a very embarrassing situation for your own titillation. You wouldn't stop when I asked you to. You were determined to get what you wanted."

"Well, now I know. Come upstairs. Let me show you I'm sorry."

August turned away and headed toward the park entrance.

Kathleen chased after her and grabbed her arm. "Don't ignore me. I can't stand that."

August looked down at Kathleen's grip on her arm. "Let go, Kathleen."

"Will you call me tomorrow?"

"I'm meeting with the police. We'll talk after that."

Chapter Thirteen

THE 19TH PRECINCT STATION of the New York Police Department was a four-story building in the middle of the block on East 67th Street. Globed lights on either side of the front door proudly displayed "19th" in gilt letters. Blackie led the way up the cement stairs and held the heavy front door for August. In the lobby, a uniformed policeman perched at a raised desk, behind a hand-lettered sign, *All Persons Must Stop At Desk.* He grinned when he saw Blackie. "Detective Rye, as I live and breathe."

"Scottie, my good man. This is Attorney Mapes. We're here to see the lieutenant."

"Sure." He gestured toward the stairs. "Go on up."

At the top of the stairs, a glass door led into the detective squad room. Instead of the dark blue beat policemen's uniforms, the dozen detectives scattered around the room wore their own version: white dress shirts with the sleeves rolled up to their elbows, slack-knotted neckties, fedoras, and guns in shoulder holsters. The room smelled of perspiration and cigarette smoke.

The detectives sat at a hodgepodge of mismatched desks accumulated randomly over the generations. Two men and a woman occupied straight wooden chairs lined up against the wall. One man was handcuffed to the chair arm. Above their heads, another hand-lettered sign cautioned, *No Spitting or Swearing.*

Blackie shook hands with the detectives all around and introduced August.

"Professor!" A giant of a man stood in the restroom doorway. "You son of a bitch, why didn't you tell us you were coming?" He crossed the room in three strides and caught Blackie up in a bear hug. His bright red hair was buzz-cut, half an inch long all over his head. He looked August up and down. "Sorry for my language, ma'am, but I'm sure you've heard worse hanging around this old reprobate."

"Attorney Mapes, this is my former partner, Arthur Quinn, but call him Ginger. I'm the best thing that ever happened to him, so excuse him if he's a little overwhelmed seeing me."

Ginger guffawed and hugged Blackie again, lifting him off his feet. "He's right, but don't let him know I said so. What are you doing here, Professor?"

"Came to see the lieutenant. Is he in?"

"I think so. Go on in."

The lieutenant was on the phone. He motioned to two visitor chairs. "I don't talk to the press. Call headquarters." He hung up. "Blackie. Good seeing you. Have you made your first million yet?"

"Not yet, Lieutenant. Attorney August Mapes, this is Lieutenant Hogan."

"Ma'am. What can I do for you today, Blackie?"

"We may have a lead on two homicides."

"In the Nineteenth?"

"Not exactly in the Nineteenth, and maybe not exactly homicides."

The lieutenant scratched the back of his neck. "You're going to have to break that down for me, Blackie."

August passed a file across the desk. "This will provide all the details, but in a nutshell, my client, a freelance book editor, appears to be in contact with a person who has murdered twice. In each case, he describes the crimes to her in writing. His victims were major figures in traumatic events in her life. We're not sure about the writer's motive for the murders or for involving my client. We worry there may be more killing in store and that my client may be in danger. The killer has been outside her apartment in the Village twice that we know of. We're also concerned she may become suspected of being somehow complicit in the crimes."

The lieutenant opened the file. "Blackie, you said these homicides weren't in the Nineteenth. Where were they?"

"Well, that's part of the problem. They're outside NYPD's jurisdiction. One in New Canaan, Connecticut and one in Mexico."

"What do the Connecticut cops say?"

"The killer made the murder, if that's what it was, look like a suicide. The New Canaan police bought it."

"Maybe it was." Hogan closed the file.

August and Blackie looked at each other. August spoke. "We realize the evidence is thin. If you'd just be willing to read the file, we'll have some place to start if there are further developments."

Hogan nodded. "I'll look over the file. You said the killer has been outside your client's apartment in the Village. I can see if the Sixth will alert the uniforms to keep an eye open. Maybe they'll turn up something. I don't suppose you have a description."

Blackie and August shook their heads.

Hogan walked Blackie and August to the stairs. "Good to see you, Professor. We miss you around the squad room." He gestured toward the glass door. "There's nobody to keep all these ruffians in line with you retired."

"Thanks, L.T. We'll stay in touch."

August and Blackie stopped on the sidewalk in front of the building. Blackie shook his head. "Not exactly full-throated support, but it's about the best we can do with the evidence in front of us at this point."

"Yes, Hogan is a good connection. We'll wait for the next development. If the past is any predictor of the future, it will come soon." August gestured across the street. "Let's go to that coffeeshop. You can fill me in, and I can tell you about my interviews with Louis and Carole Collins."

They found a booth in the back and ordered coffee.

Blackie took out his little notebook. "I tracked down the etorphine hydrochloride, but I'm afraid it's another dead end. This guy is slippery. The only place selling the stuff is a wholesale drug supply outfit on Long Island. They keep a careful accounting of the purchases, since it's a controlled substance. I'd hoped to find some record of E. Gamin buying it. No luck. The last sale was to the Bronx Zoo almost a year ago. The zoo isn't as careful as the seller about keeping close track of the stuff. They bought ten doses and could account for only one having been used on an animal, a lion who needed a tooth pulled. Nine doses are missing. The killer wrote about using one on Dan Gates and another on the priest, but we know the priest was probably killed by someone other than Gamin. If he stole all the zoo's vials, he could have eight left."

"Potentially eight more murders."

Blackie nodded. "And if he follows the same pattern, more murders connected with traumatic events in Miss O'Brien's life." Blackie flipped to a blank page in his notebook. "That's all from me so far."

August consulted her notes. "So, my visit with the aunt. She's attractive, tough, and controlling. She has no sympathy for the man who killed her sister, but the priest is an entirely different story. She believes Kathleen falsely accused him of sexual assault in order to manipulate her guardians into transferring her to a different school. Carole implied things got out of hand when the uncle threatened to go to the police. Louis put Kathleen in a different school against Carole's objections. The decision created a rift between Carole and Louis Collins that exists till today."

"Could Carole be a suspect?"

"Maybe for Gates. Unless she's sending me down a wrong path, probably not for Father Laurette."

"Could Louis Collins be a suspect?"

"Maybe. I didn't get the impression he's a killer, but I'm not a detective. I'm way out of my depth on this case, Blackie. I'd feel much better if we could get NYPD actively working on it." August was thinking not only of the criminal nature of the case, but also of her personal involvement with Kathleen.

August gathered her things and scooted out of the booth. "I have to get back to the office. Do you want to share a cab?"

Blackie shook his head. "I'm going back to the station. Maybe Ginger will see an angle I'm missing. Don't let his looks and manner fool you. He's a smart detective."

"We'd appreciate any help he can give us."

***

Lena was on the phone when August hurried in the office door. "Just a moment, please." She pushed the hold button. "It's Miss O'Brien."

August went to her desk. The scene from L's flashed through her mind, Kathleen's arm around her hips and the half smirk on her face. "Put her through." She took a slow, steady breath and picked up the receiver. "It's August."

Kathleen's voice was shrill. "He's been here again and left another chapter. I'm frightened. Can you come now?"

"Yes, and I'm bringing the names of some criminal defense attorneys. You need to make a choice."

August copied three names from her Rolodex, along with their contact information, folded the paper, and put it in her blazer pocket.

Lena looked up from her typing. "I know. You'll be back in a minute."

"This won't take long."

August crossed the park and rang Kathleen's apartment bell.

"Come up." The door buzzed.

Kathleen opened her apartment door before August knocked. She embraced August, pulled her into the room, and shut the door behind her. "You came right over."

"Of course. You said you were frightened." August removed her arms. "You have to be more careful about opening the door like that. There's a killer showing up leaving these envelopes. You need to know who's buzzing before you—"

The swish of a toilet flushing across the room interrupted August's admonition. June came through the bathroom door, barefoot and wrapped in the burgundy silk robe Kathleen had so tenderly draped around August's naked shoulders just a few days before.

June froze. "August." She wrapped the robe closer around her.

"Hello, June."

June looked from August to Kathleen and back again. "You two have business. I'll just get going." She headed across the room to the bed.

"Don't leave on my account." August watched June gather her dress and underwear and take them into the bathroom. She fingered the paper in her pocket with the defense lawyers' names and tossed it on the coffee table. "Those are attorneys you should interview to take over your case. As soon as you've chosen one, I'll brief him and make an introduction to the police lieutenant."

Kathleen picked up a familiar manila envelope from the coffee table. "Can't you just take a minute to look at this? It's another chapter. Another murder."

August sat on the sofa and took out the typed pages. She focused on her reading as June tiptoed out of the bathroom, exchanged a few words with Kathleen, and left.

My dearest Kathleen,

The enclosed story was very difficult to write. Even though the voice is first person in all the stories, I have tried to keep some objectivity about the main characters. I feel the psychiatrist is a thoroughly reprehensible individual, and I'm afraid this comes through. I hope you find the work up to your standards.
With deepest regards,
E. Gamin

Dr. Alistair Miller

I stopped at the bell captain's desk and checked the canvas bag with my tools inside. Across the lobby, an inconspicuous sign at the bottom of the escalator announced the meeting. American Association of Child Psychiatry Annual Convention Opening Banquet, Registration — Mezzanine. *I joined a crowd of men in tuxedos and women in cocktail dresses on the moving stairs. At the top, a long registration table stretched in front of the entrance to the ballroom. Three lines of people, good rule followers, sorted*

*themselves by the first letter of their last names in front of
appropriate stations. The M-R line was in the middle.*

*The women seated behind the table were struggling to keep
up with the rush. I finally reached the front of my line. "Dr. Chris
Milner."*

*The woman shuffled single-spaced typed pages showing
attendees names, hometowns, and, as I had hoped, hotel room
numbers. She glanced up with a desperate look on her face. "Did
you say Milner?"*

"Yes, M-I-L-N-E-R, Boise, Idaho."

*She thumbed through the pages more slowly and ran her
finger down a column. "Marx, Miles, Miller, Morris."*

I read his information upside down: Dr. Alistair Miller, New
York City, Room 583.

*I glanced at the growing line behind me. People were shifting
impatiently from foot to foot. "I registered a little late. Is it
possible my name didn't make your list?"*

*She looked doubtful. "Sometimes that happens." She looked
around for a person in authority to save her. The other women
were busy managing their own lines.*

"What if I come back later, when you're not so busy?"

"But you need your name badge and your table assignment."

"I'll come back. Don't worry."

*She reached under the table and came up with a ticket that
looked like one you'd get at a movie theater. "Thank you, Dr.
Milner. This will get you into the ballroom for cocktails. I don't
think anyone will ask, but you never know. Come back for your
table assignment before the program starts."*

"Oh, I will." I looked at her name badge. "Thanks, Margaret."

*Fifty round dinner tables covered with gleaming white
tablecloths, formal dinnerware, and colorful centerpieces filled the
ballroom. In the front of the room, there was a head table on a
raised platform. On the wall behind was a gigantic picture of him
and under his smiling face was printed,* Dr. Alistair Miller,
President-Elect, American Association of Child Psychiatry. *Waiters
in white jackets circulated around the room with trays of cocktails*

and hors d'oeuvres. In the middle of the room, the man of the hour himself held court. He looked more like a movie star playing a psychiatrist than a real one. White teeth a bit too big, hair a little long, a perfectly tailored tuxedo over a slender frame.

The lights in the ballroom flickered, the signal for taking your seats. He moved to find his place at the head table. I didn't need to watch the rest of the performance. Time to locate Room 583 and prepare for Phase III. I passed Margaret still checking in last-minute guests. She glanced up, and I gave her a wave.

I collected my canvas bag from the bell captain and took the stairs to the fifth floor. 583 was at the end of the hall on the left. I pulled on gloves and used the house phone in the hall to call housekeeping. "May I have fresh towels in room five eighty-three?"

"Certainly. Right away."

A maid came up the back stairs with an armload of towels. I followed her down the hall to the room and watched her knock lightly on the door. "Housekeeping." She waited for a response, then used a passkey, pushed the door open, and stepped into the room. I caught the door before it swung shut. "Thank you. Just leave them on the bed."

"But I can straighten the bath."

"No need." I slipped a generous tip into her hand. She backed out of the room, bowing the whole way.

I unzipped my bag and took out the small leather syringe case. There were two needles. The first was my usual anesthetic. I put the syringe in my pocket. The second was a new twist, aconite, though I preferred the more colorful name, wolfsbane. A fast-acting substance that causes heart and respiratory system paralysis, resulting in death. Perfect for my purposes tonight. The death looks like asphyxiation.

I wondered if Dr. Miller might be interested to know Alexander the Great was killed with wolfsbane. I zipped the canvas bag, stowed it under the bed, and looked around the room for the best place to hide. Behind one of the long window drapes would serve nicely.

I sat on the edge of the bed to wait. The traffic buzz below was punctuated every so often by an impatient honk. I ran my mental movie of the Phase III plan.

Following dinner, Dr. Alistair Miller thrills the crowd of his colleagues with an eloquent and inspiring acceptance speech in which he modestly downplays his pioneering work with disturbed children. After a standing ovation, he patiently accepts the congratulations of a long line of well-wishers then reluctantly takes his leave with a weary yawn.

He rides the elevator to the fifth floor and walks to the end of the hall. The key scrapes in the lock. He enters the room, flips on the light, takes off his tuxedo and white pleated shirt, and hangs them carefully in the closet. He goes into the bathroom and brushes those perfect white teeth. He comes back into the room and sits on the edge of the bed. I time my lunge perfectly. In the split second after the flash of surprise in his eyes and before his instinct to cry out, I plunge the needle with etorphine hydrochloride into his jugular. He falls backward across the bed.

An ambulance's wail in the street below interrupted my internal Phase III movie. I checked my watch in the glow from the street. Two minutes after midnight. Downstairs at the hotel entrance, banquet guests stood in line for cabs. I took my station behind the drape and readied the syringe. I suppressed the urge to urinate, a sure sign of excitement for me. In school, the urge often came on me just before the curtain went up.

I heard soft whistling outside the door. He was happy with the way the evening had gone. He opened the door and turned on the overhead light. I pressed harder into the wall. He kept up the whistling through his teeth and loosened his bow tie. He sat on the edge of the bed and picked up the phone. "A bottle of Dom Perignon with two glasses, please." He was expecting company.

He hung up the phone and bent over to take off his shoes. I had to move right away. I threw back the drape and jumped him, plunging the needle in his neck. He fell backward against the headboard. His head made a sickening hollow thunk. Thankfully, no blood. He had knocked the phone off the end table. I picked up the receiver and dialed room service. "Yes, Dr. Miller, how may I serve you?"

"We just ordered champagne. We need to cancel."

"Certainly. Is there a problem?"

"A change of plans."

I replaced the receiver and went to the door to hook up the security chain. Miller lay on his back staring at the ceiling with his mouth open. He was snoring. Not looking like a movie star anymore. There was a light knock on the door. I muffled his snoring with a pillow and waited. Another knock, this time louder. "Alistair?" A woman's voice. She jiggled the doorknob. Persistent. I waited. Silence. She must have given up.

I stripped off Miller's tuxedo and shirt and hung them in the closet. He had stopped snoring, but I put the pillow back over his face anyway. I took off his boxer shorts and slipped off his shoes and socks and put them all in his suitcase. I pulled my canvas bag from under the bed and lined up my tools: a plastic dry cleaner bag, a leather belt, a half-full tube of lubricant, two porn magazines, a pair of pink silk panties, and my wolfsbane syringe. I pressed his fingertips on the cleaner bag, belt, lubricant tube, magazines, and panties. Slathering his flaccid penis with lubricant disgusted me, even with my latex gloves on, but it was necessary. I smeared his right hand with the gooey stuff too and opened the magazines to the centerfolds.

Should I put the plastic over his head and then inject the wolfsbane, or the other way around? I slipped the plastic over his head and secured it with the belt around his neck. His next breath sucked in the thin plastic and caused a coughing spasm. I had to rush the injection of the wolfsbane, and I missed the jugular. I put the pillow back over his face until the coughing stopped. His breaths came in irregular jagged gasps and finally stopped altogether.

I stood back and surveyed the scene to see if I'd missed anything. I saw a flash of pink under one of the magazines. The silk panties. The icing on the cake. I worked them over his feet and onto his ankles.

I zipped my bag and went to the door. Would he have the light on or off for his autoerotic hijinks? I decided the light would be on so he could enjoy the centerfolds. I stepped into the hallway and closed the door.

August put the pages back in the envelope. "We need to find this psychiatrist and warn him. He's in danger. Who is he?"

"I have no idea who the psychiatrist might be. Couldn't you look up the professional association mentioned in the story? Who is their president?"

"Gamin usually fictionalizes the facts in the story. You told me you tried going to a psychiatrist and the therapy didn't work out. Do you know the name of the doctor you saw?"

"Do you really think the chapter could be about him? It was so long ago. I was only a child. I remember him as Dr. Aaron, but that may have been his first name."

"Where was his office?"

"Here in the city. Maybe Park Avenue?"

"That's a start. I'll get back to you."

Jane Alden

Chapter Fourteen

BACK IN HER OFFICE, August called Blackie. "Can you come to the office right away? There's another chapter. There may have been another murder."

"Be right there."

She hung up and left her hand on the phone. She considered calling Carole Collins. She remembered the aunt's characterization of Kathleen as "deeply disturbed" since she was a child. Maybe she knew more details about Kathleen's therapy. August decided to try. "Lena, get me Carole Collins at Collins Design."

"I will. June has called twice. Should I get her first?"

"No, I don't have time for that now."

A receptionist transferred August's call to Monica, Carole's assistant. August pictured the bouncy ponytail and black turtleneck. "I'll see if she can take your call. Hold on please."

"Carole Collins here."

"Miss Collins, this is a sensitive subject to discuss on the phone, but I'm afraid we have an urgent situation. Someone's life may depend on information you have."

"I assume the situation is about Kathleen?"

"Connected with her. I'm looking for the name of a psychiatrist whom she saw when she was a child."

"Go on."

"Do you know anything that might help us locate him?"

"Just a minute." She covered the receiver and gave muffled instructions to someone. August heard the office door close.

"I told you Kathleen is disturbed. I got the impression in our meeting you preferred not to hear the details."

"I did pick up on your comment. I should have been more open to hearing you out."

"Whatever. Kathleen's problems began when she was a child, at birth for all I know. It was terribly distressing to my sister. To give you some background, Francine and William married before my sister finished Barnard. She wanted only to be a wife and a mother, and she intended to start a family right away, but five or six years went by before Kathleen's birth. During the time of waiting, Francine felt desperate for a child. She and our brother became even closer. Mother was suffering with cancer, which took her finally, and it was a blessing that Louis had Francine in his life."

August pulled out her pad and pencil to take notes. "Louis told me how close he and Francine were."

"Yes, they were. The three of us were close, in our own ways."

Carole, this flinty, in-control person, sounded almost wistful. August's internal Wonder Woman reared her head. Carole was grieving the separation from her brother. Could August play a role in some kind of reconciliation?

"Francine had a difficult pregnancy, and following Kathleen's birth, the news was not good. The doctors said Francine couldn't have another baby. We turned our attention to spoiling Kathleen. She was beautiful, of course, and smart. She needed constant stimulation. Enough people were around, prepared to give her the attention she craved, so it wasn't such a problem, but as she got older, from two years old or so, she began to show behaviors that worried Francine. I wasn't around the child that often, of course. They lived in New Canaan, and I was getting Collins Design going in the city.

"One day Francine called me, sobbing. They had been banned from a play group because Kathleen pinched the other children, stole their toys, and she showed only surprise and no remorse at all when she was scolded for the behaviors. Francine wanted to take her to a child psychiatrist, but William wouldn't hear of it. He preferred to think it was just 'only child' behavior and that Kathleen would grow out of it."

August underlined *showed no remorse* in her notes. "His attitude is understandable. A proud father would want that to be true."

"Yes, but she didn't outgrow it. When she started school, the behaviors bloomed into lying, manipulating, and a lack of empathy for anyone else's feelings. Francine went against William's wishes about the psychiatrist. She secretly began bringing Kathleen to New York once a week for therapy. I used my contacts to find someone discreet who treated difficult cases like Kathleen's."

"Then your sister was killed."

"Yes, and Kathleen refused to continue seeing the psychiatrist. I had guardianship, Louis and I did, and I was in the process of getting access to information from the psychiatrist about the course of her therapy. I was scheduled to meet with him when the Father Laurette business arose. You know the rest."

"What was the psychiatrist's name?"

"Just a moment. I may have kept it. Here it is. Aaron Steinberg, M.D."

Chapter Fifteen

FOUR BLACK-AND-WHITES surrounded 615 E. 91st Street, halfway down the block off Park Avenue. The front door of the three-story townhouse was standing open. August hurried up the steps. The door led into a small waiting area. There was no space for a Lena-like person, just a few upholstered chairs, a coffee table, and a sign that said, "Please be seated. The doctor will be with you shortly."

A uniformed policeman stopped her just inside. "The office is closed."

A door leading from the inner office into the waiting area opened. Blackie spoke to the officer. "It's all right. She's with me."

She started toward the door, and Blackie put a hand on her arm. "Brace yourself. It's disturbing."

"He's been murdered?"

Blackie nodded. "As soon as you gave me the name, I started calling all his listed numbers. No answer, so I tipped Ginger off, and he met me here this morning. When we got here, the door was unlocked." He nodded toward the sign. "The doctor's first appointment of the week was sitting here, a mother and her son, patiently waiting to be called in by the doctor. He was already dead by then. The woman says she didn't hear a thing. We sent her home. The officer has been collecting addresses and turning people away as they show up."

"Is Detective Quinn here?"

Blackie nodded. "He's inside with an evidence tech and a photographer."

"Is it like the story?"

"Yes, without some of the more lurid touches."

She looked toward the door. "Do I need to see it?"

Blackie pressed his lips together. "If I were you, I would. You're going to want to close the book on this Kathleen O'Brien situation, and I would advise sooner rather than later. Now that we have a murder in their precinct, we can hand this off to NYPD and you can turn your client over to a criminal attorney. You're rightfully concerned she might be implicated in the murders. When you cut the cord, you'll want to feel closure."

"You're right, and I've taken the first step to sever ties with her." She turned toward the inner office door. "Lead the way."

Detective Ginger Quinn stood back with his hands in his pockets. He looked up as Blackie and August entered. "Miss Mapes." He took off his fedora and placed it on a carved walnut desk against the left wall. He ran his hands across his carrot-colored buzz cut. "This is something,' huh?"

Against the far wall, between two doors, was a brown leather couch. A nude dead body lay stretched its full length. If this was the psychiatrist, he was not the handsome movie star version the author described in the story. His sagging midsection and pallid skin signaled his age and a sedentary lifestyle. His head faced into the room, but the features, covered by a plastic bag, were indistinct. A flashbulb from the photographer's camera popped, making August jump. The burst of light momentarily lit up the corpse's face, the eyes wide open and the mouth gaping to suck in his last gasp of air.

August felt bile rise in her throat. She swallowed hard. An evidence tech stood over the body, dusting the plastic covering his face for fingerprints. The plastic was secured by a leather belt around the neck. The corpse gripped the end of the belt in his left hand.

She surveyed the rest of the room. There was a stack of clothes folded neatly in a chair by the couch. The desk was bare except for Ginger's hat, a telephone, an open appointment book, and a bottle of whiskey with one glass. Behind the desk, bookshelves were filled with reference texts and medical journals.

"Is it Dr. Steinberg?"

Ginger held up a black leather wallet. "According to the driver's license in his pants pocket." He glanced at the body. "The coroner will take over as soon as the tech finishes. Appears he's been dead a couple of days. We'll know a lot more after an autopsy. Looks to me like autoerotic asphyxiation gone wrong. I've seen a case or two. A guy wants to get an extra kick, drinks a little too much beforehand, and accidently does himself in."

Blackie walked over to the desk and moved Ginger's fedora off the appointment book. "Have you looked at this, Ginger?"

The detective peered over Blackie's shoulder. "What you got, Professor?"

"His appointment book. Easy enough to contact Friday's patients to find the last person who saw him alive. The last appointment was somebody named Chris Carr with an asterisk after the name." He looked at August. "What do you think the asterisk means?"

August shook her head. "No idea. It appears he makes his own appointments. No sign of a secretary. There was something special about that particular patient. One interesting thing—Chris is the killer's name in Chapters Two and Three."

Blackie snapped his fingers. "Right."

Ginger went back to observing the fingerprinting process.

August walked over to the door left of the couch. "I wonder where the door goes?"

"Let's find out." Blackie fished a pair of rubber gloves from his jacket pocket.

August raised her eyebrows.

Blackie shrugged. "What? Once a cop, always a cop." He turned the doorknob. "The door is unlocked on the inside." He pulled the door open and tested the outside knob. "Locked on the outside." Two cement steps led down to a narrow walkway between the office and the blank brick wall of the building next door. "I suppose patients can come in the front and leave through this door for privacy's sake."

August walked to the other door, on the right of the couch. It was standing open a few inches. She could see the corner of a grey metal four-drawer file cabinet. She glanced at the detective bending over the body. "May I look inside?"

"As long as you don't touch anything without gloves."

She pushed the door open with her elbow. Each drawer of two identical cabinets was labeled with sections of the alphabet. "Blackie, can you come here? Look for Kathleen O'Brien's file."

Blackie opened the drawer marked M-O and thumbed through identical brown file folders, each labeled in red in a neat hand with a patient's last name and first initial. "No O'Brien. Maybe her therapy was too long ago. Twenty years is a long time."

"I think doctors are required to keep their records in perpetuity. Check for Chris Carr."

Blackie pulled the A-C drawer open and shook his head. "Nothing for Carr."

Ginger peeked around the door. "Professor, take a look at this." He led the way to the couch and pointed to the floor. The corner of a spiral notebook was barely visible under the edge of the couch. Ginger stuck a pencil in the spiral and lifted out the notebook carefully. It was open to a page covered with handwritten notes. He read it aloud. "At the top it says, 'CC— intake interview. Young adult.'" He looked at August. "That may be the meaning of the asterisk next to Chris Carr's name in the appointment book. It could indicate a new patient, or one who was older than his usual patients."

He read on. "Well-dressed and well-spoken. Articulate, even glib. Superficially charming. Presenting complaint— Misunderstood by family and friends getting in the way of achieving true potential. Not appreciated. Not able to sustain personal relationships because women don't pay attention to anything but themselves. 'I need them to pay attention to me.' Affect naturally flat. Constantly looking for clues from me as to my reactions. Emotions seem forced. Probed any insight that others' feelings may have validity. No acknowledgment. Preliminary diagnosis—DSM/SPD. Treatment plan..." Ginger turned the page. "Nothing more. It breaks off before he detailed a treatment plan. What does DSM/SPD mean?"

August went to the bookcase behind the desk. "I think I may have a clue." She pulled a heavy volume from the shelf.

"Diagnostic and Statistical Manual. I saw this in a library." She turned to the index. "SPD is Sociopathic Personality Disturbance."

"Does the book say that an SPD is a murderer?"

August turned to the section for sociopathic personality disturbance and skimmed it. "Not explicitly. It says extreme cases are often termed 'psychopathic' and can involve physical violence."

Two men in white coats came through the door pushing a gurney. They looked around the room. "Which one of you is Detective Quinn?"

Ginger held up a finger. "That's me. Load him up."

The two men transferred the body from the couch to the gurney.

August felt the tension between her shoulder blades relax a little. Unlike Blackie and Ginger, she was unaccustomed to being in the room with a murder victim. They watched the coroner's assistants wheel the corpse through the door. "Do you get inured to it?"

Blackie shook his head. "This is a part of the job that I don't miss."

Ginger bagged the notebook, the appointment calendar, and the whiskey bottle and glass. He picked up his hat from the desk and turned to Blackie. "Thanks for the tip, pal. We should have some word from the coroner within twenty-four hours. I'll give you a call."

"Thanks, Ginger."

Jane Alden

Chapter Sixteen

AUGUST JERKED HER PAJAMA top off and threw it against the wall. The glowing dial of her bedside clock said 4:16. Sleep was impossible. When she closed her eyes, she saw the burst of light from the forensic photographer's flashbulb reflected on the plastic covering Dr. Steinberg's face. E. Gamin, or Chris, or whoever the killer was, appeared to be methodically killing people who figured prominently in Kathleen O'Brien's past. Why? How many more people would die before the police stopped E. Gamin?

She gave up trying to sleep and padded barefoot into the bathroom for a shower, as cold as she could stand. She wrapped herself in a terrycloth robe and headed for the kitchen to make coffee.

Plenty of time this morning to treat herself to French press. She lifted the glass canister from the shelf above the refrigerator. The sight of the press reminded her of June and when they were together, and the rare Sundays they allowed themselves the luxury of a leisurely breakfast.

She put water in a teakettle to heat and scooped coffee into the bottom of the press. The front doorbell rang. Who in the world would be at her door this early? She went down the stairs. The bell rang again, and she opened the door a few inches and peeked out.

June stood on the step, blowing out breaths that turned into frosty clouds. She ran her fingers through her hair. "You wouldn't answer my calls, so I came to you. I waited in the park until you turned on the light. I've been working up the nerve to ring your bell. I haven't slept."

The icy wind whipped the edge of August's bathrobe. She shook her head. "Come on in. It's freezing out here. I'm making coffee." She led the way up the stairs. The teakettle let out a shrill whistle, and August jumped to move it off the flame.

June pulled out a stool at the counter. "You're making French press like we used to."

August nodded. "I was remembering that too." She added a little hot water to the coffee, stirred it, then filled the rest of the glass canister. She checked her watch.

June laughed. "Exactly seven minutes. You are wonderfully precise."

"I haven't slept either, June, so I suggest you get to it."

"Does your not sleeping have to do with me being at Kathleen's?"

"No, there's been another murder. That makes three, and who knows how many more to come?"

"I want to explain."

August held up her hands. "There's no need. I've sworn off Miss O'Brien, and I'm turning her case over to a criminal attorney."

"Can you just listen? She called me and told me about the agoraphobia. I didn't let on you had mentioned it. She said she felt ready to trust me enough to leave her apartment with me. She suggested we go to L's. You remember, the bar over on Bleeker we used to go to?"

June paused for an acknowledgment, but August just waited.

"I tried calling you, twice. Lena took the messages. I'm not always sure she gives you my messages. I don't believe Lena quite approves of me."

"You tried calling me for what purpose?"

"I guess to get your permission to go for a drink with her."

"Lena gave me your phone messages. She is too professional to deliberately lose a phone message."

"Sorry. Well, anyway, Kathleen being your client figures into the situation too. She told me you're uncomfortable crossing the line between the professional and the personal with her. You said as much at lunch. I assumed you'd decided to cool things off. I thought you'd be okay with us just having a drink at L's."

August checked her watch again and pushed the plunger of the press. She filled two mugs and pushed one toward June.

"I certainly didn't intend to go to bed with her. We met at her place. We were leaving the apartment headed to L's when she went into a panic attack. Have you seen her have an attack? It's terrifying to watch. I can only imagine what it's like for her going through one. I wanted to call an ambulance to take her to the emergency room, but she absolutely refused. She has medication, so I found the pills for her and got her in bed. She calmed down after a few minutes, asked me to just hold her." June shrugged. "One thing led to another."

"So you stayed the night and the next day."

June opened her mouth and closed it. She sipped her coffee. "I started to say I made a mistake, but a mistake is when you can't balance your checkbook. I knew what I was doing was a bad idea, and I went ahead anyway. I expected to have a chance to tell you. I never dreamed you'd drop by."

"Drop by? I didn't drop by. Kathleen called me and said she urgently needed me to come to her apartment."

"She wanted you to walk in on us? Why would she do that?"

August flashed on Carole Collins's warning. *Be very careful of being manipulated.* "She played both of us."

"Played us for what purpose?"

"I suspect neither you nor I are professionally qualified to understand her purpose. We probably wouldn't find it very rational."

"Any wonder I prefer tax codes and spreadsheets to human behavior?" June tentatively covered August's hand with her own. "I feel I need to ask you to forgive me."

"No need. As I said, I'm unwinding things, personally and professionally, with Kathleen O'Brien. Her aunt Carole gave me some advice I'll pass on to you. Be careful of being manipulated."

The phone downstairs in the office jangled. August and June exchanged looks. "It must be a wrong number this early."

June took a last sip of her coffee. "I'll get out of your hair. I'll let myself out." She took August's face in her hands and kissed her forehead. "I love you, you know."

August caught the phone on the fifth ring.

Kathleen almost sobbed. "I got another chapter. It's about another murder."

"Read it to me."

"Here on the phone?"

"Yes."

"First there's a cover note."

My dearest,

I hope you enjoy the enclosed chapter. With your help, things are moving at a terrific pace. Here's a question: when an author begins a book, does he generally know how long it will be? I'm beginning to think this book could go on for some time. If your advice is that I should step back and evaluate how many chapters are to come, please let me know.

Yours,
E. Gamin

August shuddered.

"Should I go on reading the story?"

"Yes."

P.J. Turley

Ice boat sailing on the Hudson River is a sport for the rich and patient. There are only five or six days a year when conditions are right for an ice sail race. And that's not every year. An ice boat isn't really a boat. There's no hull. No need for one. It's more like a giant sled with sails attached. The term came from the early 1600s when Dutch settlers rigged their boats with wooden skates so they could transport livestock and supplies along the frozen river.

When the robber barons began building cottages in the Hudson River Valley as getaways from the city, they took up the sport as a way to compete with each other beyond who could amass the biggest fortune. They had ice boats built specially without hulls and with sharp metal runners. There was a time when an ice boat was the fastest vehicle on the planet. Some of them could travel seventy-five miles an hour.

The sport is dangerous. Fickle winds and crowded courses cause the boats to collide and capsize. It's not unheard of for people to be run over and killed by the metal skates. The robber barons didn't sail the boats themselves. They hired young stand-ins, much as they hired jockeys for their racehorses. I learned all this esoteric information doing my New York Times *morgue Phase I research for the P.J. Turley event.*

Nowadays, Miss Turley spends most of her time at her Duchess County cottage, writing the next best seller in her mystery series, The Dark Diva. *The books have made her rich and put her publisher, Summit Press, on the map.*

She's an avid ice boat racer. She's competitive, and she wins more than her share. She practices as often as possible when there are favorable conditions. She also loves publicity. It's good for selling books. When I called, posing as a New Yorker *columnist, she jumped at the chance for an interview about her ice racing.*

The cottage was a rambling, field stone affair, sited in a grove of trees next to a stream. The trees were bare and the stream frozen to a trickle, but I imagined it would be idyllic in the warmer months.

I pulled the rope on a bell next to the front door. P.J. Turley opened the door. She was tall and fit with short, curly blond hair and icy blue eyes.

I stuck out my hand. "Chris Frost."

She led me into a cozy paneled living room, furnished with an overstuffed sofa flanked by easy chairs around a fireplace. I rubbed my hands together in front of the fire. "That feels good."

She indicated a liquor cart in the corner. "I can offer you a drink, but I won't join you. I'm sailing this afternoon, and I need all my faculties."

"No, thank you." I looked around the room. "Is this where you write?"

"No, I have a studio out back." She sat in one of the chairs and indicated the other for me. "I don't want to seem rude, but could we move along with the interview? The wind will be best in about two hours. Catching the right conditions is key."

"Of course." I opened my bag and found my notebook. I stifled a smile when my hand brushed the etorphine hydrochloride case. "I appreciate the opportunity to interview you, Miss Turley."

She took a cigarette from a silver box on the coffee table and lit it. "I agreed because of your interest in my racing. Just about everything that can be said about my writing has already been covered. Racing is a real passion for me."

"I can tell. I've done quite a bit of research on the sport, which is rather esoteric, if you don't mind my saying so. How did you first develop a passion for ice racing?"

The interview lasted about an hour. She was animated when she described the sport, her boat, and the technical aspects of racing, but as time went along, she became more restive. The third time she checked her watch, I decided to spring the critical question for my planning process during Phase II.

"You've sold me on the allure of the sport. You're going sailing this afternoon. Is it possible I could go along for a ride?"

"If you have the nerve. Follow me to the Hudson River Ice Racing Club."

Excellent!

***

At the end of a long pier jutting into the river, P.J. and a club attendant readied the boat tethered to the pier. The canvas sail flapped and snapped in the stiff wind. I pulled my parka's fur-lined hood over my head and turned up the collar.

P.J. looked up and waved. She paced the length of the craft, double-checking the fittings. "Looks good. Go ahead and board, and I'll cast off."

I climbed into the boat. "Any instructions for the passenger?"

"Remain completely still. Balance is very important. You'll be tempted to lean with the craft, but leave that to me. Otherwise, you could tip us over."

She hopped onto the tiller seat, leaned over and loosed the line, and pushed us away from the pier. The sail billowed with the wind. P.J. knew what she was doing. She pulled the sheet so that the sail caught the stiff northeast wind. We flew across the ice toward the Poughkeepsie Bridge. The metal skates sang against the ice. I gripped my seat and focused on staying completely still. She glanced at me, threw her head back, and laughed. "You look scared to death. What a pussy! Hold on and mind the boom. We're coming about." She pulled the tiller hard toward her body. The skates chattered and the boat skidded sideways, throwing up a rooster tail of shaved ice. The boom swept across the boat. The boat tipped on one skate and for an instant it paused, then the sail filled again, and we shot off in the direction of the pier.

I yelled in her ear. "How fast are we going?"

She looked up at the small red triangle-shaped flag fluttering at the top of the mast. "Probably seventy."

We shot past the pier and ran north along the ice so smoothly that it felt like flying. I took advantage of the calm to run my internal movie of Phase III.

In my movie, I've come to the club the next day to say goodbye and watch P.J. shove off for her practice. I watch the club attendant walk away toward the clubhouse. My syringe and a short piece of cotton rope are ready in my pocket. When she takes her seat, I inject the etorphine hydrochloride. She slumps across the tiller. I tie her arm to the stick, loosen the tether line, and watch the sail catch wind. The boat shoots away from the pier toward Poughkeepsie Bridge.

P.J.'s voice broke my reverie. "We're coming about. I'll stop at the club and let you off. I want to practice some moves that are difficult to do with both of us onboard."

I nodded.

She pulled the boat alongside the pier.

I crawled over her onto the dock. "Thank you for the interview and for the thrilling ride. May I come by and watch your practice session tomorrow? That will give me another perspective for the article."

"I'm afraid not. The weather won't be cooperating tomorrow." She looked at the sky. "This northeast wind will blow in a snowstorm late tonight. We caught a brief window today."

My heart dropped. "That's disappointing." I'd have to improvise.

***

The snow P.J. predicted had begun to fall from the night sky. I wiped my gloved hand on my pant leg, readied the syringe, and rang the bell beside her front door. What if she wasn't in the house but in her studio out back? Improvisation was not my strong suit. She opened the door. When she recognized me, her expression was a mixture of puzzlement and annoyance. I stuck the needle in her neck. The drug hit her system in an instant, and she fell to the floor on her back with her legs underneath her at an awkward angle.

I dragged her to the easy chair where she sat for the phony interview earlier in the day. The liquor cart in the corner offered a choice of several expensive whiskies, but I didn't take time to sample. I picked one and poured half a glassful in a crystal tumbler and emptied the rest onto the chair around her. I pressed P.J.'s fingertips onto the glass and the bottle and set the glass in front of her on the coffee table.

I lit a cigarette from the silver box and stood it up in the crack between the cushion and the chair arm. It smoldered nicely. "Not as elegant as the original plan, P.J., but just as effective."

I took a last look around, went out the front door, and closed it.

"What should I do?"

"What is your connection with an author like this one?"

"I can't think of any. I did work at Summit Press five years ago."

"Messenger the story to my office, and Lena will send a copy back to you as usual. Have you chosen your attorney? We'll need to get the whole file to him, including this latest chapter."

"I've looked at the names. I promise I'll call them today."

Jane Alden

Chapter Seventeen

"I HAVE NEWS. GINGER called me. He has results." It was Blackie on the phone. "The coroner finished the autopsy on the psychiatrist."

August grabbed a pencil and pad. "I have news too. Miss O'Brien got another story delivered to her front door. This one's set in the Hudson River Valley."

"Holy smokes."

"Exactly. Tell me about Dr. Steinberg first."

"The doctor died at approximately seven p.m. on Friday before we found him Monday morning."

"How can they be so precise about the time of death?"

"They start with subjective evidence. In this case, the time between his last patient on Friday night and the first patient when we found him on Monday morning. Then they measure lividity, discoloration caused by settling of the bodily fluids, and rigidity of the limbs. Full rigor mortis is at its peak at fifteen hours after death then slacks off."

"What about cause of death?"

"Ginger tipped the coroner off to look for needle marks and chemicals in the body. Normally they might miss those details, especially given the indications of autoerotic asphyxiation. Accidental deaths like that happen more often than you'd think."

"It's what the killer counted on."

"The coroner found two needle marks and traces of both etorphine hydrochloride and wolfsbane."

"Where would the killer get wolfsbane?"

"I've got a lead. In the Caribbean culture it's used as a medicine. Supposed to cure colds, fever, pneumonia, laryngitis, and so on. Of course, in small amounts and taken orally, not injected into the vein. The stuff is sold in herb shops in some neighborhoods. They're called botanicas. According to my authority, the most likely source would be an open-air market called La Marqueta in Spanish Harlem."

"I'll meet you there in an hour. We can check on the wolfsbane and I'll bring the new chapter."

August took a taxi north to the market. The entrance was on 116th and the market ran south to 111th Street, underneath the railroad viaduct. Steel girders supporting the train tracks formed a roof for the stalls lining a wide pedestrian aisle down the middle of the market. August and Blackie stood for a moment taking in the garish colors of the food, clothing, and craft stands and cacophony of sounds from the vendors and crowds of shoppers. Neon signs in English and Spanish competed for customers' attention.

Blackie led the way down the center aisle. "Let's find someone to ask." They stopped at a stall with perfect, crusty bread loaves lined up behind a glass and a neon sign announcing 'bakery' in Spanish and English. Three middle-aged women wearing spotless white aprons served a line of customers. Blackie pointed to a loaf and pulled out his wallet. "Thanks. Can you tell me where I can find the botanica?"

The clerk pointed down the aisle. "Halfway down on the left. Sister Francesca."

August and Blackie joined the swirl of the crowd that carried them past a combo playing salsa music and more colorful stalls to a sign identifying Botanica Santa Inez. A large black woman wearing a brightly colored turban and robe sat on a gold chair with scarlet upholstery. She was lazily waving a smoking bundle of dried leaves. She looked into August's eyes and beckoned her into the space. August had the creepy feeling that Sister Francesca had been expecting her. Shelves held colorful candles and statuettes of saints. The walls of the stall were lined from floor to ceiling with small wooden drawers. A ladder on a track leaned against one wall.

August stepped forward. "Sister Francesca?"

"What are you seeking, chica?"

August looked at Blackie and back at the woman. "Do you sell wolfsbane?"

Sister Francesca nodded and pushed herself up from her throne. She pointed to a drawer near the top of the back wall. "I pray you will climb with your strong legs and bring it down for us. Sister Francesca is too old and fat."

Blackie rolled the ladder to the spot she indicated and climbed up.

"Just to the right. Bring down the whole drawer."

Sister Francesca sniffed the dried leaves in the drawer and nodded. "Boil for two minutes, very good medicine. Boil for any longer, very bad poison." She took a small paper bag from under the counter and filled it with the herb. "Do you know the other lady?"

August took the bag. "Other lady?"

"The other lady who came for wolfsbane."

August and Blackie exchanged a glance. "What did the lady look like?"

"A white lady. La Morena."

"A dark-haired white lady?"

Sister Francesca eased herself into her chair. "Yes. Did the medicine help her?"

Blackie took out his wallet again. "We'll ask her. How much?"

Sister Francesca gestured toward a jar on the counter filled with bills and silver. "As you see fit."

Blackie dropped two fives in the jar.

They found a coffee bar with spindly-legged tables and chairs. Blackie came back to the table with two tiny steaming cups of thick, fragrant espresso.

August opened the paper bag and sniffed the herb. "Ugh! Smells nasty." She handed the bag to Blackie. "What do you make of Sister Francesca asking about a woman? Could we have been on the wrong track all along thinking of our killer as a man?"

Blackie shrugged. "Hard to know. Could be the killer is a woman, or he may have an accomplice, or the dark-haired female customer may have nothing to do with our case."

"Carole Collins is a brunette."

"After your interview with her you felt sure she wouldn't have murdered the priest."

"Unless she was throwing me off the scent." August took a folder from her briefcase. "This is the new chapter. If E. Gamin is true to form, the next murder is looming somewhere in the Hudson River Valley." She summarized the P.J. Turley story. "The only apparent connection with Miss O'Brien is Summit Press."

Blackie nodded. "I'll go by the nineteenth precinct, let Ginger know what we found out about the wolfsbane, and fill him in on this new chapter. Hudson River Valley isn't in NYPD's jurisdiction, but they'll want to alert the local area police. In the meantime, I'll see what I can find out at Summit Press. I have a poker buddy who works in the business office."

"Thank goodness for your contacts."

"You live long enough, you know people."

Chapter Eighteen

KATHLEEN PLACED A CUP and saucer on the coffee table in front of August and filled the cup from a China pot. "What will Detective Quinn ask me?"

"He'll want to know about your connection with Dr. Steinberg."

Kathleen sat next to August on the sofa. "I won't be able to tell him much. It was twenty years ago."

"Just answer his questions directly. Don't feel you need to speculate."

Kathleen picked up the pot to refill August's cup. She jumped when the downstairs bell rang, spilling the tea. "Damn!" She ran to the kitchen for a cloth.

August followed her. "You get the door. I'll clean up the spill."

Kathleen went to the door and pressed the intercom button. "Yes."

"Miss O'Brien. It's Detective Quinn, NYPD."

"Yes, I'm on the top floor." She pressed the button and left the apartment door open a crack. Her hand shook as she took the wet cloth from August.

August searched her face for signs of an oncoming panic attack. "Just answer the questions truthfully. I'll be right here."

They heard Quinn's footsteps on the stairs, then a knock. Kathleen went to the door and opened it. Detective Quinn's big body filled up the doorway. He was breathing hard, and the color of his face matched his hair. "That's quite a trek. If I lived here I might drop a few pounds." He took off his hat, pulled a rumpled handkerchief from his back pocket, and mopped his forehead. He reached into his pants pocket for his badge, juggled a file folder he was holding, and dropped his hat. He looked up sheepishly. "Sorry." He stuck out his hand. "Detective Quinn."

Kathleen shook hands and backed away from the door. "Come in, Detective."

August marveled at the strength in Kathleen's voice. She had either managed to become eerily calm, or she was putting on a good show. "You know my attorney, August Mapes."

Quinn made a little bow in August's direction. "Miss Mapes."

Kathleen indicated a chair next to the sofa. "We're having tea, Detective. Will you have some?"

"Thank you. Thanks." He sat heavily and looked around for someplace to put his hat, deciding to put it on the floor next to his chair. Kathleen handed him a cup of tea. He took a drink, then balanced the cup and saucer on his knee and opened the file folder. "Miss O'Brien, I believe you know Dr. Aaron Steinberg of..." He checked a paper in the folder. "Of six fifteen East Ninety-first Street?"

Kathleen glanced at August. "I was the patient of a Dr. Aaron twenty years ago. I'm not sure if it was his first or last name, and I don't know the address. I was eight or nine years old at the time."

"Dr. Steinberg was a victim of foul play." He took a photo from the folder and leaned toward Kathleen. The cup on his knee rattled in its saucer and spilled the liquid over the lip. "Oops." He placed the cup on the floor next to his hat. "I wonder if you'd take a look at a photo."

August intercepted the picture. "May I look first, Detective?" The picture showed a close-up of the dead man's face, apparently on an autopsy table. August hesitated passing it to Kathleen.

Kathleen took the photo. "It's all right. I want to help if I can." She studied the face. "It could be him. He looks older, but of course he would, and he has less hair than I remember." She turned the photo sideways. "Yes, it could be Dr. Aaron." She handed the photo back to Ginger and smiled.

Ginger made a note, then took out a folded manila envelope from the file. He smoothed the creases in the envelope against his thigh and handed it to Kathleen. "I believe someone delivered this envelope and contents to you here at your apartment. That's your address, right? And the return address is E. Gamin at a PO box here in Manhattan? Do you recognize the envelope?"

Kathleen took the envelope and nodded.

"If you could remove the contents and help me understand what we're looking at here."

Kathleen shook out several typed pages. "It's the original of a chapter for a book I'm editing for Mr. Gamin. I'm a freelance editor." She looked at August. "My attorney must have told you about the other chapters. I've edited two chapters before this one, and he just delivered another."

"You say you're editing a book for Mr. Gamin. Have you met with him or spoken to him on the phone?"

"No. That may seem unusual to you, but it's not. I often communicate with my clients totally through the mail."

"How do you know your client is a mister?"

"My mental picture of him is male. I suppose the tone of his writing sounds like a man to me. Plus, the first two chapters described mysterious deaths too, so he appears to be a serial killer. Those are usually men, aren't they?"

"More often than not." Ginger made a note. "Where were you last Friday evening, Miss O'Brien?"

"I was here, working." She gestured toward the rolltop desk.

"Is there someone who can confirm that for us?"

Kathleen tapped her lips with her finger. "Hmm." She looked at August. "You and June were here Friday. Remember? You came over because he had delivered the psychiatrist chapter." She held up the typed pages.

Ginger asked again. "And later on in the day, that evening?"

"I was here, working."

"Alone?"

Kathleen nodded.

"Did you happen to have any deliveries that evening, say groceries or takeout food? Sometimes we forget those details."

"No. I would remember."

Ginger nodded. He made another note. "When was the last time you saw Dr. Steinberg?"

"It was shortly before my parents were killed. It must have been sometime in the fall of 1932."

"Twenty years ago."

Jane Alden

"Yes."

"Well, there's a lot of water under the bridge since then." Ginger chuckled and looked from August to Kathleen. He checked his notes. "Miss O'Brien, are you familiar with etorphine hydrochloride?"

"It's a strong tranquilizer used most often by veterinarians. I was very interested to learn about it in the course of editing Mr. Gamin's chapters."

"And wolfsbane?"

"Wolfsbane shows up in this story. It's a poison. Was Dr. Steinberg poisoned?"

"We're still working on the forensics." Ginger began to gather his paperwork. He leaned over and picked up his hat. "Sorry about the tea. Miss O'Brien, this is embarrassing, but I wonder if I could use your facilities? I rushed over here not wanting to be late and all."

"Of course." Kathleen led him across the room to the bathroom. She looked at August and raised her eyebrows.

August signaled her to keep quiet.

Kathleen gathered the cups and the pot and took them to the kitchen. They heard the toilet flush and water run in the sink, and Detective Quinn came out of the bathroom.

"Thank you for your cooperation." He handed Kathleen a card. "Call me at the station anytime if you think of something that might help us." He tipped his hat to August. "Counselor."

Kathleen saw him to the door.

He took a step, then turned. "One other thing, Miss O'Brien, are you planning a trip out of town anytime soon?"

Kathleen glanced at August. "No."

"Good, good. Thanks again for your help."

Kathleen closed the door behind him and leaned against it. "I think that went well. He doesn't seem very bright, does he? I expected Joe Friday from *Dragnet*, but he's more like his dumb partner."

"The private investigator I work with knows him well. He advises not to underestimate him. Which brings us back to the

132

subject of getting you good representation for a criminal matter. Have you made a choice?"

"I've talked with each of them by phone." Kathleen went to the desk, raised the rolltop, pulled the paper from a cubbyhole, then closed the rolltop. She tossed the list on the coffee table. "I'm not impressed with any of them." Kathleen took hold of August's blazer lapels. "I'm going to insist that you remain my attorney."

August encircled Kathleen's wrists and moved her hands from the lapels and held them at her sides. "That's not going to happen, Kathleen." She shrugged into her topcoat. She picked up the paper from the coffee table. "The sooner you settle on one of these, the better. I can brief him about the situation so far."

Kathleen reached for the list. Her hand shook so hard it made the paper crackle. She swayed against August, and her knees buckled under her. August held her as she collapsed onto the sofa.

"Are you all right?"

Kathleen's hand fluttered to the scar on her forehead. "Some water, please."

August filled a glass in the kitchen and brought it to the sofa. Kathleen took the glass, but her hand was too unsteady to raise it to her lips. She began breathing in short, ragged gulps. She grabbed August's forearms. "My medication. It's in the drawer next to the bed."

August ran to the bedside table and jerked open the drawer. A heavy black object slid against the front of the drawer. The gun Kathleen's uncle bought her. August found a vial half full of blue pills. She rushed back to the sofa.

"Open it. Open it." Kathleen shook three pills into her palm and tossed them down her throat.

August went to the phone. "I'm calling an ambulance."

"No, no. Just get me in bed. I'll be all right now. The pills always work."

August helped her across the room to the bed and under the covers. Kathleen's breathing had steadied some, but still came in short gasps.

"What else can I do? I think I should call an ambulance."

"No, no. I've tried that before. They don't help. It makes me feel more anxious and out of control. If you can just stay with me till the pills start to work. I'll sleep for a while, and when I wake up, everything will be back to normal."

August sat on the side of the bed. Kathleen sighed deeply, closed her eyes, and smiled. She grasped August's hand and held on tightly. "I know you need to leave. As soon as I'm asleep, you can go."

"Just relax."

Kathleen's grip on August's hand began to loosen as she nodded off. Her hair spread on the pillow, baring the jagged scar along her hairline. She sighed and smiled again as she drifted deeper into medication-induced sleep. She whispered indistinctly, and August bent down to hear. "I've always known you're special. You're different from other women. You pay attention to me."

A memory flashed in August's mind: Detective Quinn standing beside the psychiatrist's nude dead body, reading aloud notes from the intake interview of a new patient, Chris Carr. *Not able to sustain personal relationships because women don't pay attention to anything but themselves. "I need them to pay attention to me."* Quinn, Blackie, and August assumed they were notes from the interview of a male patient. What if Chris was a woman? And what about the Chrises in the other chapters? Sister Francesca said a dark-haired woman bought wolfsbane.

August stood and looked around the loft apartment. Her eyes landed on the rolltop desk. She checked the steady rise and fall of Kathleen's breathing, kicked off her shoes, and tiptoed across the room to the desk. The rolltop was closed, but not locked. She slowly slid the top open. There was a portable typewriter with a grey plastic dust cover over it. Beside the typewriter were neatly stacked pages. August picked them up and read.

Carolyn Wright

Sandwiched between two snowstorms, the first week of December brought unseasonably warm weather to New York City. Perfect for my plan.

I found a parking spot directly across 89ᵗʰ from Claremont Riding Stables. The paradox of a horse barn in the middle of the upper west side of Manhattan made me smile. When it was built in 1892, the three-story building served elite New Yorkers as an old-time parking garage for buggies and horses, before cars. In modern times, it morphed into boarding stables for equestrian hobbyists who rode their horses on the bridle paths in Central Park. Carolyn Wright boarded her horse there.

I jaywalked and knocked on one of the big green stable doors. A short elderly man in scuffed boots and a flat tweed cap pulled the door open and stuck out his hand. "Come on in. I'm O'Connor." The place smelled of seventy years of horse manure and hay, not altogether unpleasant.

"I'm Chris Rogers. We talked on the phone."

"Yes, you're the friend of Miss Wright?"

"More a professional acquaintance."

"She's a regular. She rides three mornings a week at the crack of dawn, Monday, Wednesday, and Friday, rain or shine." He took off his cap and scratched his head. "So you're looking to board."

"I'd like to take a look around. I'm just beginning to consider next steps."

"I can show you the place. The first floor here was originally carriage storage. The customers use it now for storing saddles and tack. The horses are on the second floor. Third floor is groom bunks, offices, and whatnot."

He pointed toward a rickety freight elevator in one corner of the cavernous space. "The horses go up and down in the elevator."

We took the stairs to the second floor. Four ranks of stalls held horses, some standing, some lying down, all waiting for their masters. Two teenaged boys brushing down horses glanced up at us.

"We board about fifty horses. Used to be double that before the war. Business is coming back slowly." He scratched the forehead of a horse in the nearest stall. "One day, the real estate will be more valuable than the business. I hope to be gone by then." He led the way down the line of stalls. "Miss Wright's horse is down this way." He stopped in front of a big, black horse with a shiny, healthy-looking coat. "This is Bella." He petted her nose and the horse nuzzled his hand.

"She's a beauty."

He looked me up and down. "What breed did you say your horse is?"

"I haven't exactly bought a horse yet. It's a big step."

"We're pretty picky about the horses we board, or I should say we're picky about their owners. We want to stick with serious riders who exercise their horses regularly. Of course, we can arrange for workouts when our owners are out of town on business or whatever."

"You could call me a serious novice."

"Well, that's okay. We all have to start somewhere. We keep a list of instructors we can recommend, if that would help."

I reached toward Bella's nose. "Is it okay if I pet her?"

"Sure." He fished in his pants pocket and handed me a piece of carrot. "Give her this."

Bella's nose felt like velvet and her breath was hot on my palm. I wondered if horses had a sense of time passing, and if Bella was anxious to see her beloved mistress.

O'Connor gave Bella's head a final scratch. "Well, I need to get back to it. Some of my owners will be coming in from their workouts. If there's anything else I can show you, or if you have more questions, you know our phone number."

"I'll be in touch." I followed him down the stairs.

***

The next week, I tracked Carolyn's early morning workout three final times to satisfy myself the routine never varied. On the *third morning at 5:30 a.m., before dawn, I parked down the block from her apartment building. At six, she followed the night shift doorman out of her apartment building's front door on 5th Avenue. She looked handsome in her beige jodhpurs and tall brown leather riding boots. I couldn't help admiring the strength and grace of her stride. Before I started studying her to prepare for Phase III, I never fully appreciated the athleticism of a serious horsewoman.*

The doorman hailed a taxi for her, and I followed it up 5th Avenue to the 86th Street cut-across of the park, then north again on Central Park West. I circled around and parked on 89th, across from the stables.

I pictured Carolyn riding the creaky freight lift to the second-floor stalls area and Bella, stomping and whinnying, anticipating her workout.

I checked my watch. Saddling up usually took her about twenty minutes. While I waited, I pulled my canvas duffel bag into my lap to check my tools: a syringe case with two needles full of etorphine hydrochloride, a hemp rope, heavy suede gloves, and rubber wading boots. I stashed the bag in my trunk. It would wait there for Phase III, only a few days away. The wide street-level doors of the stables swung open. I followed on foot as she led Bella down the block, across Central Park West at the crosswalk, and into the park. She mounted and headed south on the bridle path, as always. She would follow the path circling around the reservoir then north to the very top of the park, a wooded area named North Woods.

The architects who designed the park in the late eighteen hundreds wanted to give the average New Yorker a respite from the stress of nineteenth-century city life. The remote section at the northern tip had tall trees, streams, and waterfalls. You'd swear you were in the Adirondacks. Perfect for my plan. The area was deserted at that time of the morning.

I checked my watch again. Her circuit around the reservoir and through the park would take half an hour. I turned left and jogged directly toward the North Woods. Fifteen minutes later, I arrived at a footbridge spanning a running stream, deep in the woods. I looked over the low banister at the rushing water. Even in the slightly warmer weather, sheets of ice lined the stream's banks. I closed my eyes and ran through my mind movie of how Phase III would unfold in a few days.

August shuddered. It was the unfinished story of the next murder victim. She searched the desktop for more pages, then took the dust cover off the typewriter. There was paper in the roller. At the top on the left-hand margin, *Page 3,* then the continuation of the story.

Running through the scenario in my mind's eye, I arrive at the bridge and check my watch. Plenty of time to set up. I open my canvas bag and change into wading boots and pull on the heavy gloves. I tie one end of my rope to the trunk of an overhanging tree across the bridge on the north side. I use a bowline knot, a kind of slip knot, perfect for my purposes. NOTE: I learned to tie a bowline in Scouts. I once won a dime by being the fastest to tie the knot with my eyes closed. I move across the bridge to the south side, paying out the rope so it lies slack on the floor of the bridge, and take my hiding place behind a shrub. I grip the end of the rope and wrap it around my gloved fist twice.

The sound of the steady clip clop of Bella's hoofs on the bridle path changes pitch as they reach the wooden bridge. Just as Carolyn rides by, I stand up and jerk the rope, the knot around the tree trunk tightens, and the rope pulls taut. The rope catches her waist-high and clotheslines her clear out of the saddle without harming Bella, which I have been very careful to avoid. Carolyn lands on her back on the rough boards of the bridge. As she lies stunned, I inject her, pull her down the bank and into the icy water facedown. Some lizard brain instinct for survival takes over her body, even though she is heavily sedated with the etorphine hydrochloride, and she begins to struggle. I'm forced to hold her down with my knee in her back...

A metallic click echoed across the loft. August turned to face Kathleen standing beside the bed holding a gun pointed at her head.

"That sound was me cocking the hammer. It loads a bullet into the chamber. All I have to do is pull the trigger. Move very slowly. Put the cover back on the typewriter and close the desktop."

August complied.

Kathleen indicated the desk chair. "Now sit." Kathleen walked over and sat on the sofa. She braced her elbow against her knee so the gun pointed steadily between August's eyes. "Well, this is a fine kettle of fish, isn't it?"

August motioned toward the typewriter. "What does this mean, Kathleen?"

Kathleen smiled. "I can almost see the wheels turning in your brain, putting all the pieces together. Now I have a legal question, and how you answer is very important. Since you're my lawyer, if I lay it all out for you, you have to keep it confidential. Attorney/client privilege. Right?"

"That's a complicated question, but in general, yes."

"Good, because I think you deserve to know the whole story. You've been so helpful to me. I meant what I said. You're special."

Jane Alden

Chapter Nineteen

KATHLEEN KICKED HER SHOES off and pulled her legs underneath her. "Settle back. This is a long story." She rested her hand with the gun on the sofa arm and kept steady aim at August. "First of all, I did not murder David Gates. I assume he killed himself, just as the newspaper said. I'll admit, over the years I've had fantasies about doing away with him. His drunk driving the night he killed my parents was not just an anomalous episode. He was an alcoholic who continued to drive and put innocent people in danger. I kept track of all his arrests.

"If things had gone on much longer, I might have actually acted on my fantasies. When I heard he had committed suicide, I felt disappointed, robbed of the possibility of ridding the world of him myself. That's when I wrote the story. Just for my own enjoyment, a sort of purging of emotion."

August noticed the irony of Kathleen's choice of words. Far from showing 'enjoyment' or "emotion," her affect was eerily flat, emotionless. The gun never wavered. The barrel looked as big as a cannon. August shifted in her chair. "I could use a glass of water."

"Of course." Kathleen smiled. "You might prefer wine. There's a bottle open in the refrigerator, but I'm afraid you'll have to help yourself."

"Water is fine." August went to the kitchen and filled a glass from the tap. She returned to her seat by the desk. "Where does E. Gamin come on the scene?"

"After I finished writing the story about David Gates, I began to think of it as more than just one story. What if it were a chapter in a book about all the people in my past whom I needed to pay back for the traumas they've caused me and those I love?"

"You mean you started planning to murder them."

"Well, I couldn't expect all of them to cooperate by committing suicide, could I? The purpose of E. Gamin was to divert attention away from me, of course. I made him up and mailed the story to myself. I needed help because of my condition, and I found you, thanks to June.

"You even helped me make my writing better. Do you remember the first time we met? I showed you the David Gates story and asked you what you thought of the writing. You said the main character seemed to move through the world as though he were invisible, without human interactions. You were right. After that, I tried hard to connect her with other characters in the stories."

August felt equal parts revulsion and fear grip her stomach. She drank the water. Maybe she could use the glass somehow as a weapon if she could find an opening.

"What about Father Anthony?"

"Technically, I didn't murder the priest. He was all the way down in southern Mexico. There would be no way to get down there without using public transportation, which isn't possible for me right now. With a little research, it was fairly easy to find someone for the job. Father Anthony had managed to make himself unpopular with certain people. Plus, he was probably up to his old tricks with little girls. It was only a matter of time before his sins caught up with him."

The grandfather clock struck half past the hour. What hour would that be? August tried to gauge how much time had passed since she walked across the park from her office to Kathleen's apartment for the appointment with Detective Quinn. She figured about two hours. "So Father Anthony did molest you at the school?"

"Again, not technically, but Louis believes things were headed in that direction. The priest was grooming me. And in a way, Father Anthony did penance for all the priests who have abused helpless children. Louis was abused. You could look at Father Anthony's death as payback for what happened to my uncle."

August shifted in her chair. "Put the gun down, Kathleen. I want to listen to your story, but it's difficult with a weapon pointed at me."

"I can't do that, August. Get some more water. That will make you feel better."

August shook her head.

"Where was I? Dr. Aaron. He was a charlatan. He had my mother and Aunt Carole completely fooled, but I saw through him right from the start. The whole thing was Aunt Carole's idea. Mother and I went into the city every week. It was such a waste of our time. Mother waited outside reading magazines. Dr. Aaron watched me play with dolls and draw pictures while he made notes. My father didn't know we were seeing the doctor, and Mother made me promise not to tell. Dr. Aaron was the cause of my mother and father's death as much as David Gates."

"I don't understand."

"I'll show you. Look in the top desk drawer."

August slid the drawer open. Inside was a brown file folder labeled in red, *O'Brien, K.* It was the therapy record missing from Dr. Steinberg's filing cabinet. Beside it, in the corner of the drawer, was a sharp blue pencil, the kind Kathleen used in her editing work. In one motion, August lifted the file folder and scooped up the pencil. She opened the folder on her lap and hid the pencil under her thigh.

"Inside you'll see a record of weekly visits over a span of six months. They end when my mother was killed. I refused to see him after I came out of the hospital. Read for yourself. It's in the notes from the last meeting. He called me a psychopath. Can you imagine telling a mother that her beloved nine-year-old daughter is a psychopath? The anguish his pronouncement must have caused her. He was in it for the money, of course, and he was jealous of me because I was obviously smarter than he was.

"The night my parents died, we were driving home very late from visiting my grandmother. I was lying down in the back seat. They thought I was asleep. They were arguing. My mother told Father about Dr. Aaron and about the visits we were making every week. He was furious. 'How could you do this behind my back? I've told you before. There's nothing wrong with her. She's an only child, and we spoil her. She'll grow out of it.'

"My mother began to cry, and then she told him. 'The doctor says she's a psychopath. He says there's no cure.' That's when the car hit us. My father was always very careful and in control. If he hadn't been distracted, the accident never would have happened. He would have seen David Gates running the red light and stopped to avoid the crash."

August closed the file folder and put it back in the drawer. "So you wrote the story about the psychiatrist, and then you killed him with wolfsbane."

"Yes. I made an after-hours appointment as though I were a new patient, under a false name. I had to convince him to see me. He usually works with children. I told him my problem started when I was a child. I half expected him to recognize me from twenty years ago. Often people remember my hair. But he was clueless. Halfway through the appointment, though, he began to suspect he might be in danger. He excused himself to go to the phone. I had to move fast, but everything turned out fine in the end. Are you sure you wouldn't like another glass of water?"

August shook her head. She calculated how many strides were between her chair by the desk and Kathleen on the sofa. At least three, maybe four. Too far to avoid being shot before she could overpower Kathleen. She needed to keep her talking until she could figure out what to do to save herself.

The clock struck the hour, eleven o'clock.

"What about P. J. Turley?"

"P.J. Turley—a made-up name, of course. You've always been curious about my panic attacks. They started five years ago when I had to leave Summit Press. I got a job there right out of school. It wasn't much of a job, the bottom of the ladder. I was a 'slush pile' reader. Manuscripts come in over the transom, unsolicited, and they get dumped in a windowless office. When I started, they had been building up for months. They covered the floor, the desk, the chairs. I organized them by the date stamp when they arrived in the office and started reading. My boss was an assistant editor, a real bitch. I asked her what I should do if I found a good one. She just laughed.

"But I did find a good one, a murder mystery by a woman, Nell Baines, who was a writer for a comics company. I showed it to my boss, the bitch, and she showed it to her boss, the most successful editor at Summit. They told me to get in touch with the author and ask her to come in for a meeting. They signed her, and the editor promoted me to assistant editor on the spot, working with Baines. There was a long way to go. She had been writing comics for a long time, and she had a lot to learn about writing a novel. The problem from the beginning was that she wouldn't pay attention to my advice on how to make her book publishable. She took constructive criticism personally. She complained to my boss and got me fired. That's when the panic attacks started. So you see, it's her fault I have agoraphobia. Because of her."

Kathleen massaged her elbow, and the point of the gun barrel wavered.

August put her hands in front of her face. "Put it down, Kathleen. You don't want it to go off accidently."

"Oh, don't worry. I'm very competent with it." She shifted in her seat but kept her aim.

August's mind raced. She needed to keep Kathleen talking while she figured out some way to convince her to lower the gun. "What happened with Nell Baines's book?"

"That's the delicious irony. Nell Baines's story never got published. I could have made her successful and celebrated, as I have many writers in the last five years. She's living in a sad little apartment in Hyde Park, not even a comics writer any longer."

Kathleen put her finger on her lips. "I haven't yet figured out how to make the trip to Hyde Park, but I think I'll be able to soon. My agoraphobia is getting much better. You can tell it is. I passed a big test the other day. I actually went to a crowded public market in Spanish Harlem to buy the wolfsbane, and I had no sign of a panic attack."

So Kathleen was La Morena in a wig. August swallowed a feeling of panic. Keep your wits about you, Wonder Woman, if you want to get out of this mess. "And what about the story in the typewriter?"

"It isn't finished yet. It's only my first draft. You probably can tell the story is about my Aunt Carole. She is a heartless, cruel person. I told you she was responsible for my mother taking me to Dr. Aaron, which led to the car accident. She put me into that awful school against my will and over Louis's objections. Then she turned her back on us. A break with her was fine with me, but Louis has suffered because of it."

"Can you put the gun down, Kathleen?"

"I want to." Kathleen sat forward on the edge of the sofa. "We can go back to the way things were. You can stay my attorney. I'll finish my book, and we can put that behind us." She rested her hand in her lap, for the first time taking her aim off August. "We can even go to Lake Placid to the cabin you love so much. We can go canoeing on the lake, just as you described."

There was a knock on the door.

The gun came up again. Kathleen mouthed, "Quiet."

Another knock, this time louder and more insistent. "Miss O'Brien, it's Detective Quinn. Open the door."

Kathleen's attention shifted to the door behind her for a split second. August's fingers found the sharp pencil under her leg. She leapt from the chair and launched herself at Kathleen, screaming "Ginger!" She sank the point of the pencil in Kathleen's wrist with all the weight of her momentum and desperation. Kathleen reflexively jerked her hand back at the same time she pulled the trigger. August felt the bullet whiz past her ear. She fell backward, pulling Kathleen on top of her. The door broke open with a loud crack and Ginger, Blackie, and a uniformed cop burst into the room.

Ginger kicked the gun out of Kathleen's hand, and it skidded across the hardwood floor. He lifted Kathleen to her feet and pushed her backward onto the sofa.

Blackie helped August sit up. She put her hand to her ear, and it came away bloody.

Blackie pulled back her hair. "You got nicked." He handed her his handkerchief. "Put some pressure on it."

Ginger turned to the uniformed cop and pointed at Kathleen. "This one's bleeding too. Call the medics." He found a towel in the kitchen and wrapped it around Kathleen's wrist. She looked dazed. Her normally pale skin was ashen, and she breathed in shallow gasps.

"Give me a minute with her." August sat beside her on the sofa.

Kathleen began to cry. "It was an accident. I didn't mean to shoot you. I only wanted you to listen."

"I know."

"I'm sure you'll still say you can't be my attorney anymore."

"No, I can't."

The paper with August's recommendations for criminal attorneys was on the floor beside the coffee table. Kathleen picked it up. "You decide which one will be best for me."

"I will, and I'll call him and brief him on your case. He'll meet you at the police station."

"You'll tell them I didn't mean to shoot you, right?"

August nodded. "I'll tell them."

"And will you call my Uncle Louis? Just tell him there's a misunderstanding, and I'll talk to him soon."

The medic arrived with his black bag and cleaned and bandaged both the women's wounds.

Ginger told the uniformed policeman to take Kathleen to the 19th precinct station.

August pictured the crowded, stuffy squad room. "Wait." She went to the bedside table and found the blue pills. "She may need these." The policeman led Kathleen out the door.

August's ear was beginning to throb. She sat down on the sofa. "How did you and Ginger know I was in trouble?"

"Lena called." He snapped his fingers. "I need to let her know you're safe. She was worried to death."

He placed the call and came back to join August on the sofa. "She's relieved. I didn't mention the ear. You'd better tell her that in person. Anyway, as I was saying, she was worried so she called me. You missed an appointment, which she says you'd never do if you could help it. I called Ginger. He was at the station writing up an affidavit for a warrant to come back and search Miss O'Brien's apartment."

Ginger yelled from the bathroom. "Here it is." He came out holding something in his handkerchief. "I saw it in the trash when I used her facilities after the interview. It's an empty vial of etorphine hydrochloride."

Chapter Twenty

LOUIS AGREED TO MEET August in the Palm Court at the Plaza Hotel at 4:30. On the phone, she told him the bare minimum, that she needed to speak with him about Kathleen and that it was not a discussion to have over the phone. He was already there when she arrived, at a table as out of the way as possible. The waiter seated her and took their orders. "Right away, Mr. Collins."

"You're a regular here."

"It's a good place to court donors for the museum, which I spend most of my time doing these days. It's fancy enough, but doesn't take as much time as a dinner."

"You're a busy person. Kathleen has told me as much. Thanks for meeting me on such short notice."

He leaned forward. "Why are we here, Miss Mapes? What do you need to tell me about Kathleen?"

"First, I have a confession. Your sister will be joining us. I took the liberty of inviting her. You both need to hear about Kathleen. When we met in your office, you told me you, Carole, and Kathleen should be close, supporting each other. The time has come when your support for Kathleen is going to be critical."

Louis leaned back in his chair. "Does Carole know I'm here?"

"No."

"She may not stay once she sees me."

"She may surprise you. I hope she will, but of course she's free to go, as you are."

August glanced at the tearoom entrance. Carole approached the maître d', smiled, and shook his hand. She was wearing her customary tailored black business suit with a scarlet scarf at her neck. From across the room, she exuded confidence and physical grace. The maître d' led her to their table.

August saw just a flash of surprise on Carole's face when she recognized Louis, but she recovered her poise and kissed him on both cheeks. "Louis." She shook hands with August. "Miss Mapes." She took the chair across from Louis next to August.

Thankfully, the waiter appeared to take Carole's order, a welcome distraction while they all got their bearings. Louis and Carole looked at August.

"Thank you both for coming. I have some very difficult news about Kathleen. She has been arrested. I spoke with her attorney just an hour ago, and he told me—"

Louis interrupted. "I thought you were her attorney."

Carole put her hand on his arm. "Arrested for what?"

"She has confessed to the murder of Dr. Aaron Steinburg."

Carole put her head in her hands.

Louis sputtered. "Ridiculous! Who is Dr. Aaron Steinburg?"

Carole sat up straight. "Her therapist, twenty years ago." She turned to August. "Tell us all of it."

"I can tell you she was booked around noon today at the nineteenth precinct." She handed each of them her business card. "On the back, you'll find her attorney's contact information. He's expecting your call. He's excellent. Smart, diligent, and an expert in criminal defense, which I am not. I've briefed him on my work with Kathleen and turned over my files to him. Beyond that, I'm constrained by attorney/client privilege from telling you more. I'll just say she needs both of you badly right now."

Louis stood up. "I'm going to her." He turned toward the door.

"Louis, wait. I'll go with you." Carole caught up with him and took his arm. Together, they rushed across the hotel lobby toward the front door.

Chapter Twenty-one

AUGUST STOOD AT THE floor-to-ceiling great room windows, gazing through the velvet night at Christmas lights in the village across the lake. A brisk wind from the north blew snow from the branches of the white pines and made the red and green village lights appear to twinkle. To her left, she could barely make out skaters circling Lake Placid's little sister, Mirror Lake, frozen solid since Thanksgiving. Lake Placid in winter was like being inside a gigantic snow globe.

A log in the fireplace popped, sending sparks chasing each other up the chimney. The sound made August jump. The scene outside should have been soothing, but she felt restless and unsettled. "Do you want another cider?"

June put down the book she was reading and stretched. "Too sweet, but I'd love a brandy."

"Coming up. For you, I'll even break out the good stuff." August went to the liquor cabinet, filled a snifter, and delivered it to June. "Madam."

June took the glass and tasted. "Excellent." She picked up her book again.

"What are you reading?"

June held up the book. "*The Children's Hour.*"

"Why are you reading that depressing thing? Isn't that the one where she hangs herself because she discovers she's gay?"

"Shoots herself, I think. Lillian Hellman is directing a revival on Broadway, and I have two tickets. I'm thinking of inviting a fascinating new woman I met the other night at a cocktail party. One of those arty lesbians you talk about. She's a sculptor, a fairly successful one, I think. I'm studying up to dazzle her with my thoughtful critique of the play."

"What was so fascinating about her?"

"You'll think I'm shallow, but she reminds me of Francine O'Brien, my long-ago crush in New Canaan. She looks a little like her, and she has the same personal magnetism."

August turned back to the window. She leaned her forehead against the cold glass and watched a cloud drift from north to south across the face of the moon. "We'll have snow tomorrow."

"Good. I hope we get snowed in." June lifted the snifter. "If you have plenty of this brandy."

"More?"

June nodded. "Please."

August refilled her glass and turned back to the window. "I went with Carole and Louis Collins to visit Kathleen at the state hospital last week. The brother and sister have reconciled. That's one good thing that came out of an otherwise awful experience."

"How is Kathleen doing?"

"Surprisingly well. They let her start a creative writing class. She organized some of her students to read their work for us. It was quite good."

June swirled the brandy in her glass. "I've been wondering about Kathleen's agoraphobia. Do you think she really suffered from it, or did she use the panic attacks when they suited her?"

"Both. I think her panic attacks were genuine, and I think she used them to manipulate people. She used a panic attack to get you into bed."

June groaned. "Are you ever going to forgive me for my bad judgement? You're not being entirely fair. You told me you intended to keep things strictly professional with her, and don't forget, I did try to call you. Twice."

"And you said my friendship was more important to you than Kathleen O'Brien."

"You must believe my intentions were good."

"You've heard the saying, 'The road to Hell is paved with good intentions.'"

June put her book aside. "Let's not bicker. Come here, August. Come sit in my lap like you used to."

"I'm too heavy."

"You'll never be too heavy." She opened her arms wide. August settled in June's lap and laid her head on her shoulder. June kissed the top of her head and smoothed her hair. "You said the Collins brother and sister's reconciliation was a good thing that came out of the experience, but the best thing is it's brought you and me closer than we've been since we broke up. How long has it been since you sat in someone's lap?"

"Since you and I were together."

"Exactly. You are too busy rescuing everyone else to let someone take care of you."

"Lena takes care of me."

"Yes, but she takes care of you like a mother. I mean like a lover. I know what you're thinking, staring out that window. You're wondering if you could have done more for Kathleen. You did the best you could for her. Her problems started long before we knew her, but we'll never forget her. You don't forget something like that experience. Besides, if you do start to forget, you'll always have this perfect little nick out of the edge of your ear to remind you. She could easily have killed you."

August pushed up from June's lap and went to stand in front of the fire. "I'm not sure I did the best I could for her. I let my urge to rescue her get in the way of my better judgement. I let Kathleen draw me into her dark drama, and my help just enabled her to keep it up." She rubbed her hands together to warm them. "I've made a resolution. No more Wonder Woman rescues. I may not be able to control the urge, but I can resist acting on it."

June sat forward with her elbows on her knees. "But your empathy is one of your most admirable traits. Not to mention, it's a large part of how you make your living. Don't you rescue all those cheated-on wives?"

"There's a difference between providing competent and caring legal representation and pandering to my need to be needed."

"How do you tell the difference?"

"Believe me, I can tell the difference. Wonder Woman always winds up feeling tired, resentful, and used."

June settled back in her chair. "I'll make a resolution too. In fact, I've been thinking about this for a while. I'm going to cut back on my hours at work. Who am I kidding? The old boys' club at HGL is never going to make me a partner, no matter how huge my billings are."

"You're changing firms?"

"Oh, no. I won't give them the satisfaction. I've been grooming two very smart junior associates. I'm enjoying the role of teacher and mentor. The tax department will keep chugging along, and I'll take more time to have a life. Here's another saying, 'No one ever thought on their deathbed, "Gee, I wish I'd taken more meetings."' Maybe you and I can spend more time together. Maybe you'll go with me to see *The Children's Hour*."

"I think you'd better stick to your original plan of inviting the fascinating new woman. You and I can get together for French press afterward, and you can tell me all about it."

"I suppose I'll have to settle for that, if you say so." She fiddled with the dustcover of her book. "We can help each other stick to our resolutions, can't we?" She looked up hopefully. "Deal?"

"Deal."

THE END

About Jane Alden

Jane Alden was born and raised in a small Mississippi River Delta community in Arkansas. Everyone in town knew everyone else—their parents, and their grandparents before them. Though her father was a life-long cotton farmer, the family lived in town rather than on the farm, the only class difference in the all-white, all-protestant hamlet.

After graduating from the University of Arkansas, she moved to California and taught seventh grade English in a small central valley citrus-farming community. When she was recruited on the phone at U of A, she looked up Porterville, California, on the map, and it was only about an inch and a half north of Los Angeles, but it turned out the culture was closer to Arkansas or Oklahoma than to the bright lights and big city she craved. After two years teaching, she moved to Los Angeles and began a career in health care management. After many lucky circumstances and thanks to wonderful mentors, she ultimately became Chief Executive Officer at Los Angeles Children's Hospital, a mountain-top experience. After running a big organization for eight years, she became an executive coach, working with successful executives who want to be better leaders.

Jane and her partner of thirty years live in a small town thirty miles east of metropolitan Los Angeles. Claremont is rare for a Southern California town, having a distinct downtown village area and discernable city limits. Their chocolate lab, Delilah, is the captain of the domestic ship.

Visit Jane's website at janealden.com to chat about lesbian stories, our experiences, and other interesting things. 'Like" her on Facebook at Jane Alden, email Janealdenauthor@gmail.com.

Email: janealdenauthor@gmail.com
Twitter: @janealden5
Facebook: JaneAldenBooks

Note to Readers:

Thank you for reading a book from Desert Palm Press. We appreciate you as a reader and want to ensure you enjoy the reading process. We would like you to consider posting a review on your preferred media sites and/or your blog or website.

For more information on upcoming releases, author interviews, contest, giveaways and more, please sign up for our newsletter and visit us as at Desert Palm Press: www.desertpalmpress.com and "Like" us on Facebook: Desert Palm Press.

Bright Blessings

Made in the USA
Columbia, SC
04 August 2021

42897874R00089